Elfed In New York
Fugitive

D1518395

Erik Schubach

FIRST EDITION

ISBN 9798390204764

Chapter 1 – Downtime

"Kia?" Lisa, my best friend prompted. I shook my head to clear it as I looked up over the mug of sinfully decadent hot chocolate I was sipping, letting it flow over my enhanced taste buds as we watched the small television I had on top of my dresser.

I shifted to get more comfortable on our warm and breathing backrest, my family's big old sheepdog, Barney, who was gently snoring with Lisa and I propped up on him on my bed. Turning back to watch the Princess Bride I scrunched my head to my shoulders. "Sorry, just thinking about how insane the past month has been since we got back from Bangkok."

She nodded slowly and shared, "Yeah, it has been kind of hectic since you blew up the International Elf Council... again. But you said yourself that you've already seen some changes for the better in the way the Council does business, especially with the Dearmadta."

I squinted an eye in mock pain. Yeah, that was me in a nutshell, Killishia Renner Riicathi, a thorn in the side of the Council I had a seat on since my clan, the Riicathi, thought long dead, had reemerged, with two one thousandth of one percent of voting shares in the Mírë... the combined wealth of the voting families in the Council.

When I was seated in the Council after I Elfed live on network television, it was thought that my mother and I were the last of the Riicathi clan, and it would likely die out with me as I wasn't planning on having children, especially because of my disposition as the only Halfling in existence. Until my presumed dead grandparents showed up in a spectacular fashion that is.

There have only ever been two other Halflings in all the history of the Elves, as most mothers and babies died in childbirth, mom and I almost died when I was born too. The Council as recently as almost three hundred years ago, tasked the Riicathi clan, or Pallbearers, to dispatch any Halfling children and their parents who had survived, lest the Elves be discovered by the people of that era.

My family resisted the order and was almost wiped out in a bloody battle since we had been treated like indentured servants even though they held a minuscule amount of voting shares, but were never allowed a seat on the Council. The small handful of Riicathi who survived, exacted a huge toll of lives on the Elvish Security Forces... fifty-seven Riicathi had defended against four hundred soldiers and very nearly succeeded. And when it was over, and the seven remaining Riicathi cowed, they were sent out to do the deed.

The lookouts at the harbor reported the last of the Riicathi had boarded a ship heading out to the New World early that morning.

They were hard-pressed to keep the secret that Elves walked among men without their clan of assassins doing their dirty work for them. And the Riicathi had been hiding from the Council ever since. I've come to learn that their treatment of my clan had been the Council's greatest shame.

I didn't know any of this until after I Elfed, thinking I was 'human' until then. Though Elves are just as human as the rest of the population, we're just a different branch of the Homo-Erectus tree. Where there had been three branches, Homo-Sapien, Homo-Neanderthalensis, and Homo-Aelftus. Only Homo-Aelftus continued to thrive after the decline of the Neanderthal.

I guess I should start at the beginning, the day there is actually a holiday for now, Reveal Day.

It was nearly twenty-two years ago, I was just four at the time, but I remember the mix of excitement and fear from all the adults in the neighborhood, when Evander Laun and Natalia Havashire went on the air throughout the world on almost every news channel simultaneously, to reveal to the human race that Elves walked among us.

It is the most-watched historical event in modern times. We had to study it in Social Studies in school. I must have seen the clip a septillion times, which everyone at first thought was some sort of publicity stunt by the CEOs of the two most powerful corporations in the world when before our eyes, their ears lengthened to points and eyes deepened to that almost glowing blue right on the air.

There were varied reactions to this, most were skeptical and thought it was simply digital visual effects, but some governments and militaries started to react and mobilize in ways that told the world it most certainly wasn't just a corporate stunt from the two companies that reviled each other. And when more and more people stepped forward with those pointed ears and blue eyes, all mesmerizingly beautiful, the panic began.

That's when the genius of the way they chose to reveal themselves to the rest of us began to sink in. By making themselves known to all, it was harder for the government to keep a lid on it as some people panicked while others celebrated the discovery. And of course, there was the fact that the governments of the world made the realization that the companies that supplied over forty-five percent of all the arms and sixty percent of all consumer goods in the world were owned by the emerging Elvish families, which stopped any talks of rounding them up until the threat could be properly assessed.

It seems that not all the Elvish families wanted the Reveal, as the complex hierarchy of their sociopolitical society is still not entirely clear even after two decades. Whether the outliers still wished to evade discovery from Homo-Sapiens – Humans for lack of a better word, or from the influence of larger Elf families, they remained hidden after the Reveal.

They haven't revealed how they've eluded discovery all these thousands of years, when it was clear, with their pointed ears and unnaturally blue eyes that they weren't entirely like the majority of the population. Hell, we still didn't know just how many of them there were in the world, but estimates put them at a population of around a hundred million, or roughly one percent of the world's population.

There's speculation that they somehow possessed some sort of magic to hide their obvious differences from the rest of the population, though scientists dispute that theory, saying there has to be an answer in science and biology. Their genetic makeup is so close to ours that it is almost indistinguishable. Closer even than modern humans to neanderthal.

Though we've learned over the years that the tiny shift in their genetic makeup gives Elves better strength, reflexes, and senses, especially hearing than the rest of us, and because they have much denser telomeres they enjoy not only a lifespan of almost three times longer than non-elves but appear to be all prime physical specimens.

The children of the families that remained hidden after the Reveal have sometimes reached their physical maturity from between sixteen to twenty years old at inopportune times, causing their Elvish traits to manifest in public view instead of them being confined to Elvish campuses children had been confined to in the past before the Reveal. And most never shared their heritage with their children, so it was a shock to even them.

Over the past nineteen years, seemingly random young women and men would spontaneously manifest Elvish ears and eyes. And with the now overwhelming popularity of Elves in our society, they are treated like celebrities or royalty. It is viewed and celebrated almost like winning the lottery. The term people have adopted for this public manifestation was called Elfed.

A large number of young people prayed they'd be one of the lucky ones to be Elfed, and so many tried to emulate them, almost like some sort of warped worship, down to publicly wearing family sashes and pointed ear guards the Elves wore. Some went as far as getting cosmetic surgery to make their ears pointed, though they wind up quite stubby compared to real Elves.

And that was just the tip of the iceberg. Whenever an Elfing occurs, the two largest families always clamor against each other to take the new Elves under their wing and identify their family if their parents weren't forthcoming with their lineage.

The new Elves would be offered the world, and whisked away to private schools, or given jobs in the corporations to ensure they never want for anything. The most stunning of them are always given public-facing positions to woo the public with their glamorous looks. It sounds like a fairytale come true, but honestly, I was so relieved when I passed the maturity threshold to find I was just a normal human. It was because I saw what Elfing did to people.

After my public Elfing, my mother thought it was time for the Riicathi to once again step out of the shadows. And to my shock, we were seated on the Council by Evander Laun and Natalia Havashire, the two most powerful houses on the Council.

Now I wonder if they regret doing that since all I've done since I was seated is to turn the Elf Council on its head, making waves and leaving chaos in my wake. Especially since I formed the Riicathi Consortium while at the Transparency Conference in Bangkok so that I could give the nonvoting clans the Council called the Dearmadta, or more vilely the 'nulls', a voice in the affairs of the Elves which they have been denied since the Reveal.

I vote my mind on any of the issues brought up in the weekly Council meetings, unless it would affect the world's population of Elves including the disenfranchised Dearmadta, then I vote what the majority of the Dearmadta wish.

And I swear to the Great Spaghetti Monster in the Sky that whenever I do, it sends over half the hide-bound Council into apoplexy. Not to mention that the perpetually deadlocked votes over the past three hundred years, have placed me in the precarious position of having what they have never had, a tie-breaking vote. If it is something positive for all Elves and the communities we live in, I will vote, however, if the issue at hand only benefits a specific clan or group of clans, I abstain so they can enjoy that deadlock they seemed to be so determined to have before.

I'm not popular in the Council... save a few families who think it is time to shake things up like the Walkers, and to my surprise, the Launs and Havashires themselves.

And my latest innovation is being met with a mixed bag of reactions.

Since there have been records of the Council, which was originally formed to manage the Mírë, but somehow morphed into the leadership of all Elves.

But there were thousands of other minor non-voting families under them across the world.

The Mírë is like a retirement plan of riches for elder Elves when they reach a certain age. It sounds like some sort of ancient pension plan or social security set up thousands of years back to me.

The voting shares had originally been distributed evenly across all of the Elvish families, but over the centuries, voting shares of the Mírë have been bought up by more powerful families, with a promise to still allocate funds to the clans they

purchased them from if they pledge their family's allegiance to
the buyers.

In more modern times the most powerful families, the Launs
and Havashires, leveraged even more control of the Mírë by
creating contracts with a hundred and fifty of the families that
wouldn't sell. The two major families are assigned as voting
proxies in the contracts in exchange for a tiny percentage of the
Laun or Havashire wealth as Elves of the clans retire. But of
course, along with giving away their votes by proxy, they also
had to swear allegiance to the clan that secured the contracts.

There are only twenty holdouts, and they make up the
Conclave of the International Elf Council, being the only voting
members besides the controlling dual majority. Half are loyal to
the Launs and a half to the Havashires.

The voting shares were originally to dictate the best ways in
which to grow the wealth of the Elf community and keep it
hidden from the Sapiens and their governments. But it has
morphed into their ruling body.

The system has always worked well for votes about keeping
the Elvish community safe. But the unintended power struggle
between the Laun family and the Havashires is that once all the
shares were bought up, they each control exactly fifty percent of
the accounted for shares. And since the two families are
diametrically opposed, they are stalemated on any other votes or

special interests of either side. And in the past three hundred years, they have only agreed upon a single thing, and that was the Reveal.

And I just made a motion to dissolve all the contracts and proxies and return the Council to a true democracy again. There was chaos in the Council, and Evander almost had to call in security to quell the Council Members who were all shouting in anger at the suggestion.

That is, until Council Member Dieadra, of the Walker clan, spoke, her Australian accent carrying, "The Walker clan seconds the motion."

That caused another round of shouts. And I noticed that the gallery of non-voting houses behind my Council seat between the two opposing sides of the Council, all were shouting in enthusiasm, most cursing their ancestors who had sold away their shares.

Once order was restored, a thoughtful-looking Dimitri Havashire looked over to an equally thoughtful-looking Evander and Marcillia Laun, and with a slight inclination of Marcillia's head, Dimitri pounded his gavel.

"Miss Riicathi's motion has been put to the floor and seconded, but as this is something unprecedented, the Council will need to consult the legal pool, to determine if this is something that can even be voted upon. We adjourn until two

Fridays hence, to research this... decidedly volatile subject. In the meantime, go home, contemplate this on your own, and have an enjoyable Valentine's Day with your families."

I muttered under my breath, even though I knew every Elvish ear would hear me, "Renner." Dimitri looked amused at my pout.

So here we are a week later, and I took some time off from my day job at WTRL as a part-time investigative reporter... probationary, so I could spend some downtime with Lisa and my girlfriend, Tana... yes, Tanaliashia Laun, Evander, and Marcillia's Hello Kitty, goth punk princess of dreamy Elf. And I wondered just what Tana had planned for tomorrow, our first Valentine's Day together. I voiced it, "So, no clue what Tana has planned for me?"

"Even if I knew, I'd be bound by Elf, Sapien confidentiality, Killiaser."

I snorted. "No such thing woman, and stop the act that you can't pronounce my name already, you've already been busted on that." She grinned like a loon, not looking repentant in any manner.

"Speaking of tall, dark, and dishy, where be your girl already?"

I smirked and winged a thumb to my second-story window here at my family's row house. And the sash lifted and Tana stepped in holding two large pizza boxes and a big bag, a toothy grin appeared on her face as she set the bag down to shut the window against the blast of chilly February air that had Barney grunting and snorting before returning to his snoring, and me shivering.

Lisa shook her head as she shimmied to make room for Tana between us, "That's so freaky how much better Elf hearing is than us Sapiens."

I admitted as the bounty was unceremoniously dropped onto the bed and Tana crawled between us, fist bumping Lisa and giving me a peck on the lips, "I smelled the pizza before I heard her climbing." Then I cocked my head. "And how did you climb up here holding all of that? You do know we have a front door, love."

She winked at me, and shared, "Trade secret. Now, what are we watching?" She turned to Lisa who was opening the boxes to inhale deeply the tantalizing aroma of Vinnie's pizza. "Pass me a slice, woman. Plates, utensils, napkins, and drinks in the bag."

Lis and I turned to her, furrowing our brows, "Plates, utensils?" I added, "Heathen."

My badass girl blushed a little. "So sue me. It isn't my fault we had to eat our pizza on plates and with a fork and knife when I was growing up."

Lisa snorted and shoved the point of a slice in Tana's mouth as she was defending, and teased, "Poor little rich girl, never taught the proper way to consume Cthulhu's greatest gift to us, mere mortals."

We all laughed and I said in a conversational tone, knowing my mother's Elf hearing would pick it up downstairs, "Pizza is here if you and Dad want any."

Mom chuckled. "Cyrus is cooking me up something special, but thank you. And Tana? Kia is right, we do have a front door."

My cocksure girlfriend sounded like a chastised teen instead of twenty-six. "Yes, Mrs. Renner." And we all chuckled. I snuggled into my girl to watch the masterpiece of sarcastic cinema that was the Princess Bride, as we munched on the delectable pizza that Lisa handed out. Barney miraculously came back to life to snarf up the piece of sausage I placed on the pillow by his nose before nodding off again.

This was the most relaxed I have been since the day I Elfed at the Christmas Tree Lighting at Rockefeller Center in December. So I just soaked it in, knowing it wouldn't last.

Chapter 2 – Followed

It was close to midnight by the time we finished watching the Princess Bride and Grosse Pointe Blank, the two most romantic movies in my opinion in honor of the holiday of cupids and hearts. The rumble of a tank-sized vehicle approaching from a couple of blocks away had me telling Lisa, "Your Elf arm candy is here. Why didn't he come for the movies again?"

She chuckled. "The reasons are apparently twofold, miss nosy. The first is the huge dust cloud you created in the Council meeting has caused the Walkers to go into damage control since Issac's mom seconded your motion."

Tana snorted. "Yeah, you're real popular in our home right about now too, Killy, Mom and Dad have been in non-stop meetings with dozens of families who are either pressuring them to either allow or deny allowing a vote on the topic. And they have an army of lawyers outside of the Council, advising them about how it would affect our seat on the Council and the Havashire's seat."

She shrugged and absently played with one of her silver lip piercings, sharing, "Seems a lot of people are up in arms about nothing, since with or without all the proxy votes and bought shares, we and the Havashires still hold the largest block of voting shares, so will still hold control of the Council. But if all the families affected will regain their votes, this is going to obliterate the voting deadlock we've been in for so long."

Lis nodded. "Yeah, that. And second, he was prepping whatever he has planned for him and me for our first Valentine's Day together."

I really liked Issac, he treated Lis like a princess and ignored all the other Elves who looked down on dating a Sapien. I liked his family too, as they seem progressive and willing to shake the tree to see what falls out, as they've demonstrated twice now by seconding my controversial motions at Council meetings.

Tana asked her, "Give a girl a ride? I had a family car drop me off, and my security detail is still looking for me in the West Village."

As Lisa nodded, I asked, "Running away from the scene of the crime?" Showing my pouty lower lip and pointing at it just in case it wasn't apparent.

She snickered and stole a kiss, holding my cheeks to gaze into my eyes, causing my cheeks to heat and me to tuck some of my straight red hair behind an ear as I tried not to get lost in her crystal blue eyes... the same crystal blue eyes shared by every Elf except me, since as a Halfling, mine were the brilliant emerald of my Sapien father. "No, I just want to get out of here before the clock strikes midnight. Because then it will be tomorrow, and I want the first time I see you on Valentine's Day to be me picking you up at your door tomorrow night at five."

"Oh... ok," I agreed distractedly until she let go of my face and winked at me. The wench was just going to heat me and leave me in this aroused state. She may be evil, but at least she is my evil.

I sighed and shared, "I have to be up at o' too damn early anyway, I promised dad I'd help him inventory Gertie before he heads into the city to set up."

Gertie is our family food truck, where my dad makes the best Mediterranean food in Manhattan. I've been feeling guilty lately that I've been so insanely busy with Council business since I was seated there, that I haven't been able to help as much as I should. But this time off has given me the chance to rectify that a little.

The Humvee stopped at the curb and I grinned when Issac said, "Beep beep."

"Sending your troublemaker out, Issac. You take good care of my bestie tomorrow."

"Of course."

Lisa moved her finger back and forth from me to the window. "That's still disconcerting." She grabbed the last slice from the decimated pizza boxes and moved it in a follow-along gesture to my girl before kissing me on the cheek as she passed then took a big bite. How in Tartarus does she keep her figure, eating like a logger?

Tana started for the window and I grabbed her hand to march her to my bedroom door, to her grinning pleasure, the scamp. We kissed a kiss of promises of more to come and she skipped down the stairs to catch up with Lisa, calling back, "See you tomorrow night Killy. Love ya."

I held onto the edge of my door and tried not to sigh as I watched her butt sway down the stairs. "Love you too, goodnight."

Then I stepped backward, spread my arms wide, and fell back onto my bed, reaching up to wrap my arms around Barney, who opened an eye in annoyance his beauty sleep was interrupted. "G'night big guy." Satisfied, he quickly went back to dreamland. I yawned so wide my jaws ached then decided he was on to something there, and I snuggled in and joined him in dreamland seconds later.

And just as I had intoned, all too soon I was moaning at the sound of my cell vibrating on my nightstand as my alarm was going off. I felt as if I hadn't slept more than a minute or two. I used to do this every morning since I was twelve or so? I yawned, and stretched, feeling Barney rising and he sort of flowed off the bed and then trotted downstairs where I could smell coffee brewing and dad moving around down there.

I shuffled into the bathroom and took a quick shower and brushed my teeth before venturing down, calling to mom as I passed their bedroom on my way to the stairs, "Morning, mom."

She grunted in response, pulling her sleeping mask down over her eyes. I always thought she was a little eccentric for using a sleep mask until I found out she, well and I, were Elves, and our eyes are super sensitive to light. This reminds me, I needed to get online and order one for myself on LaunBay sometime. It would help with the morning headaches I got from the light sensitivity.

It felt almost nostalgic as dad and I bantered as he drove to the new storage unit to re-stock the supplies for the next couple of days as I did a spot check on the inventory. I mentioned, "You'll need to order more beef, chicken, and lamb too, dad. We're running awfully low and the stock sheets show we're almost out in the freezer in the storage unit. You're playing it close to the wire, why haven't you restocked already?"

He chuckled, but I've learned to hear the worry he hid when times were lean, winters were always a drain on our resources and bank balance, "Good catch Itty Bit. I just haven't had your keen eye keeping me on task for the past couple of months. Things have been hectic."

I squinted an eye and pulled up the company banking app on the LaunPad and winced at the paltry sum. We had some emergency funds from our family Arwë draw on the Mírë after the bulk of it was used to catch us up on bills and repair both Gertie and mom's beat-up little 1957 Volkswagen Beetle.

Then I squinted my other eye as I pulled up my bank account, preparing to wince, but was pleasantly surprised to see that instead of seventeen dollars and twelve cents like yesterday, the station had finally reimbursed me for my expenses in Bangkok with my automatic paycheck deposit, then there was the little bit I had tucked away into my attached savings account from the same Arwë draw.

I started to transfer the balance of that nest egg into the family account but dad was always two steps ahead of me. "Don't you dare move your money into the main account, Itty Bit." I stopped mid-swipe and exhaled in exasperation.

He just shared in his almost always positive attitude, "We'll weather the winter like we always have. April is just around the corner and our sales will virtually double. It's a cycle and you know it."

"I know, but it doesn't mean I have to like it." Then I remembered something I had one of the lawyers for the Council check into for me that could eliminate one of the expenses that ate away at the daily sales... the Vendor-Tax as we called it, tongue in cheek. Which is the daily parking ticket issued by our friendly neighborhood parking enforcement officer. The city refuses to give us food truck vendors any permits to park at meters, nor a dedicated place to park our rigs for customers to come to. So we're forced to park over the legal time limit and they ticket us each day as we try to scrape out a living.

I needed to get a ride back home anyway, and I've learned the subway I've ridden my whole life is a little scary for me now that I've Elfed with all the extra attention it pulls my way, some in an uncomfortable way from Elf stanners, or worse, lecherous stares.

Normally, since my ears gained their pointitude, I'd just bum a ride off my bestie or my girlfriend. But since Lis is busy with her man, and Tana is busy setting up for tonight, I'd go to Laun Tower and as much as I hate to do it, I'd get a ride home from Cliff in the Council carpool or from the Cookie Twins... the extremely pale, Russian man mountain Elves assigned to me for security who were tailing us by a respectable block and a half even now.

It would give me a chance to sneak in to see Aldrich Ingels, the lead counsel for the, well for the Council, and see if he was able to find anything out for me.

Once we restocked the mobile kitchen on wheels, we headed across the river on the Queensboro into Manhattan, from where we lived here in Jackson Heights in Queens. And we had a hell of a time squeezing Gertrude in at our normal spot by Rockefeller Center, some new truck has been horning in between our spot and Krazy Kay's Wings since December, and hasn't learned the hard lesson yet that newcomers need to respect the established food trucks' territory. In our case, all two hundred square feet of it in front of two parking meters.

The guy's truck was adorned, unimaginatively, with a single word, Burritos, painted on the side under his pop-up window. Dude seriously needed to think about branding. Like Gertie here let everyone know proudly, coming from any direction, that this is Cyrus' Mediterranean Cuisine. Everyone swears that dad's shawarma is the best in town and I've heard more than once, people on the street saying, "Let's hit Cy's for lunch."

Nobody is saying, "Let's go get burritos at, umm, Burritos." Gah, I know I sound bitter, but it is the family business, and dad has earned the respect of the other trucks and they watch out for his chosen spot as he does theirs. Krazy Kay had tried to keep the guy from parking there by encroaching a bit, but that just caused the guy, whose name we still didn't know, to encroach on our spot.

It was the boldest he's been in a long time since the day dad confronted him about taking known vendor's spaces. And my dad? Well, he's six foot four and about two hundred pounds of muscle, and intimidating as hell when his virtually always present smile drops. And with his Elf caliber of good looks, even though he is my Sapien parent, Lisa keeps informing me, no matter how many times I implore her not to, "Your dad is a grade A prime specimen of man, Kia." Just... eww.

I stuck around until we had the grills fired up and the food prep done, then hopped over to him as he put on his 'Kiss the cook' apron, and tippy-toed a kiss on his cheek. "Love ya pop. See you at home tonight... hmm or so, since I don't know what Tanny has planned for me. Gah, speaking of, I still have no clue what to get her for Valentine's Day and it is already here."

Chuckling, he told me as he opened the back door for me, letting a blast of frigid air in, causing my silver ear shields to chill even with the warm fur lining, "Love you too, Itty Bit. You're worse than your mother with last-minute shopping. I'll see you at home... whenever you get there."

I pulled a knit cap on, tucking my ears under it, and looked at the offending food truck just inches from our back bumper. And even though I'm one of the most clumsy people you will ever meet, I'm also graceful as an Elf. Well, I am an Elf, but you know what I mean. And I've recently found that there may be a reason for my apparent clumsiness. My neurons are firing Aelftus fast, but my Sapien half can't keep up with the signals, causing me to move erratically at times.

Though when adrenaline hits my system for some reason, I can keep up more with what everyone is saying. Even the Cookie

Twins say that in times of stress, I move faster than any Elf they've seen.

This though was kid's play. I hopped out, a foot on either bumper and closed the door as I pulled my mittens on. Reveling over the fact that my arm cast was finally gone from where I broke bones on the one occasion I tried to punch someone... but that's a different story. I wiggled my fingers in the mittens which I get teased for, but they keep my fingers warmer than gloves, then I took two steps and went to leap onto the sidewalk.

Well, that was the plan, but of course, I'm the butt of someone's jokes, possibly Loki since I always felt if the Norse Gods were real, Loki would mess with everyone, he is the trickster after all. Of course, no amount of grace can help a person when they step on some ice on a Burrito truck bumper.

I pitched forward as my foot pitched back. My arms were moving before I told them to and I was cartwheeling off Gertie's bumper to land knee-deep in a snow mound that had been shoveled away from the newsstand on the walk.

I looked around to find the woman at the stand, good-naturedly holding up seven fingers. I felt my cheeks burn and I shrugged at her. Then I looked at the offending truck as the guy propped his counter window up. I called out, "Hey buddy, show some respect to us regulars and not so close next time."

He snapped back, "It's Bobby, not Buddy, sweet cheeks. And I am a regular."

Before I could correct the presumptuous man, and instruct him of the difference between two decades and two months, dad came out Gertie's passenger door to just look past me to the man, and asked calmly, "How did you just address my daughter?"

The twenty-something man with the van dyke beard paled and said quickly, "Sorry Mr. Renner, I didn't know she was yours." Then he closed the window he had just opened to hide away in his truck. Dad winked at me and stepped back into the truck as I extricated myself from the mini snow bank and slunk away down the sidewalk, head down and not meeting anyone's eyes as I headed off toward Laun Tower in the twilight of dawn.

I sighed at the sound of the car pacing me, Ivan and Pietor were as watchful as ever. New York was my town, I navigated it just fine without them until I Elfed. Then I did a doubletake and stopped walking and looked at the light-ish morning traffic on the road, then hustled across to the black SUV as it pulled over to the curb.

I looked into the sole occupant as he lowered the window, the man's Russian-accented voice colored in concern as he went into hyper-alertness, "What is it, Miss Kia? Trouble?"

Shaking my head I pointed at the empty seat beside him. "No trouble, Pietor. Why does everyone automatically assume I attract trouble? No, Mr. Funnyman, Where's Ivan? I don't think I've ever really seen either of you without the other before."

"Nyet, he was called to supervise the search for the fugitive wanted for extradition to Ethiopia." I blinked dumbly, and he added, a tone of suspicion coloring his deep rumble, "You did read the Council briefing yesterday, da?"

I squished my lips to one side. "No da... nyet. I'm on vacation, I haven't read any of the dozens of messages people have sent me since the last Council meeting was recessed."

He sighed heavily and said, "When do you ever? Get in from the cold, I will drive you to your destination."

Shaking my head I beamed a smile at him. "No, I'm just going to Laun Tower." I indicated one of the two towering skyscrapers just a few blocks away, Laun Tower opposing Havashire Spire across the street from it. "And I think the city is gorgeous in winter. I'll walk unless you're too bored being alone."

He chuckled. "Alone? Nyet." He winged a thumb at another SUV parked at the side of the road just a block back, I could see two big Elves in it with my Elvish eyesight that's just a little better than a Sapien's. Ah. Well, either of the Korsivair Cookie Twins was worth any two other guards, so it made sense if Ivan was pulled away. I knew the brothers had been in Elvish Special Ops once upon a time, so his expertise must be needed for this manhunt Pietor is talking about.

I shrugged. "A little overkill isn't it?" I turned to look for a gap in traffic and hustled back to the other side to continue my trek as he assured me that no, it wasn't overkill, to which I informed him, "Drama queen," just to receive a snort from the usually not very chatty man, it was his brother, Ivan who was the loquacious one of the two... once you make your way past their stoic professionalism.

As I walked, I felt a little bit of unease, like I was being watched by more than my overprotective security detail. I surreptitiously glanced across the street again as I passed by a business center, and saw in the reflection in the window, someone was pacing me about thirty yards back. Even though the first-floor windows were almost mirrored I couldn't see their face as it was deep in the shadow of the hoodie they wore, hands jammed in their pockets. I wasn't sure if they were male or female in the baggy hoodie and jeans.

I wasn't sure what unnerved me and made me think they were the reason for my feeling of being watched, as the sidewalk, while still early morning, was starting to fill with people hustling about to get to work or to head home after a night shift. Manhattan was waking. I realized what it was that had me on edge, the way they moved. A little too fluid and precise, it reminded me of how the Cookie Twins moved with their decades of martial arts training, that ruled out an Elf stanner.

At that moment I caught Pietor's attention in the car with my eyes and almost undiscernible, nudged them back toward the watcher, and his eyes snapped over scanning the people on the walk, the person was gone. There was no place for them to have gone, there were no alleys and this was a heavy business district with the headquarters for the International Elf Council.

I wound up second-guessing myself when Pietor turned back to me and shrugged, making me second-guess myself. Had it just been just another person heading to work? They must have entered one of the offices on the street level here. I shrugged back at the man, then continued to my destination.

As I moved into the shadow between the two looming Elf towers, headquarters to our landless Sovereign Nation, the doorman at the entrance to Laun Tower was, as always, already standing at attention at the doors. Ursula looked sharp in her winter uniform, the heavy wool overcoat brushing the tops of her shining boots was immaculate, and her long swept-back ears tucked up under the wide brim of the doorman's hat. She raised one of her white-gloved hands to wave as I approached.

I waved back. "Hey lady."

She opened the door for me and inclined her head. "Miss Riicathi."

I rolled my eyes at her amusement since I've told her on many occasions to call me Kia or Killishia. She stubbornly refuses, getting some amusement from my reaction to her being so formal. Even though it was frustrating, I liked her, she was good people.

I marched right up to the front desk, the lobby only having a few early risers moving about in it, as well as a group of others, both Aelftus and Sapien, sitting in some of the posh seating areas scattered about as they waited for various appointments with representatives of the various departments housed in the skyscraper.

I didn't recognize the young man manning the desk, it seemed they rotated people through awful fast, just when I get used to seeing someone new and getting to know them peripherally, there was always someone new shortly thereafter. Or was there a pool of them and they rotated? I'd have to ask, I'm always curious about things like this.

Smiling at the Elf as his eyes widened in recognition of who I was, I started, "I guess I could have called ahead, and it is pretty early for him to be in but is..." I trailed off when I glanced back at the sound of the door opening again, and I saw past the distinguished, silver-haired elf with ebony skin and crystal blue eyes, that person in the hoodie standing across the street in front of Havashire Spire, hands jammed in the pockets of the jacket, facing my way.

But when the door closed, distorting the view for but a moment, the person was gone, and the front counter worker was prompting in question, "Miss?"

I shook my head and turned back to him. "Sorry. Is Aldrich Ingels in his office with the legal types?"

"Just a moment, let me check." He typed something on the smart surface of the desk and nodded to himself. "Ah yes, he is, shall I have him buzzed down to... Miss Riicathi?"

I was already heading to the private Council elevators behind the screen wall of the front desk, "It's Renner, and no, I know the way."

When I arrived on one of the floors staffed by the massive legal department, in stark contrast to the sedate pace of the lobby, the place was filled with Elves rushing around everywhere, dozens of conversations, and frantic calls out to others for source materials. I haven't seen the legal beagles, or is it eagles? I know it's not Sméagols since most of the lawyer-y types wouldn't know a Lord of the Rings reference if it hit them right in their Mordor.

I noted the man I was looking for was not in his office but in the bullpen, his suit coat off, tie untied, and his normally immaculately pressed dress shirt rumpled, with the sleeves rolled up as he read from a paper file in one hand, and cross-referencing something on the LaunPad tablet computer he held in the other.

His ebony complexion looked ashen, and his face looked drawn as if he hadn't slept in a couple of days. I looked around as people rushed around me like I were a piece of furniture in their path, then I scurried over to the man, feeling like I was a teenager sneaking in late after my curfew for some reason.

"Umm... hi, Aldrich, is this a bad time?"

He almost jumped at my voice but restrained himself, I hadn't meant to startle him. "Miss Ri..." He paused at my expectant look. "Kia. Yes, it is a bad time, but I don't foresee there being a better time in the near future."

He handed the file and pad off to a woman who stepped up with a stack of papers in her hands, "Get this to the security committee, it's rough and we'll refine it, but it will give them the start of a basis for possible grant of sanctuary."

"Yes, Mr. Ingles."

Then he was guiding me to the corner where there was an honest-to-goodness water cooler beside a cabinet that held a top-end coffee and espresso bar, various empty takeout containers, pizza boxes, and a mostly empty box of donuts by an overflowing garbage can. I had to ask, "What in the name of Monty Python is going on here?"

Chapter 3 – The Laramer Bloc

He blinked at me, almost in incomprehension as he poured a twenty-ounce cup of coffee for himself and motioned to it then me. I nodded and he poured me a more human size amount of the brown liquid ambrosia. Then chuckled to himself. "I forget who I'm talking to at times. I take it you didn't read the emergency briefing to the Council?"

I bit my lower lip and gave a pained look. "Not so much. But half my security detail was pulled away, Pietor Korsivair said it had something to do with an Ethiopian extradition request?"

He nodded, asking, "You know about Ethiopia and the Reveal?"

I nodded slowly, trying to recall my high school classes that covered the Reveal and what little I knew about the Accords before I Elfed. "After the government coup directly following the Accords, Ethiopia followed the Laramer Bloc, the few countries that passed anti-Elf legislation, banning them from their countries, even though they had been living there among the rest of the population all along."

I furrowed my brow and continued, "Some of the Laramer countries started shooting Elves on sight as they started trying to figure out if there was a way to test for Elves in hiding if they weren't manifesting their Elvish traits." I remember that even though I wasn't the biggest Elf fan back then, it still angered me that those five countries' bigotry and xenophobic beliefs were justifying them to either expel their citizens or even purge them from the countries with violence and death. They were still people, still human, and how could human beings treat others that way?

I sighed into my cup before taking a sip and finishing, "The freshly signed Accords had a mutual defense clause in them back then. The ink on the signatures on the Accords hadn't even had a chance to dry when the International Elf Council rallied their extremely well-armed security forces, with weapons they didn't even sell the various militaries of the world, called on the signatory nations of the Accords to pressure the Laramer Bloc countries to cease hostilities against Elvish citizens, and allow them to depart unharmed... under threat of military intervention if they harmed a single Elf."

Aldrich nodded slowly, satisfied with my understanding as he waffled his hand, "More or less. It's a lot more nuanced than that, but it's the basics."

He drank deep from his cup, gulping the hot liquid, then reached for the donut box, and motioned his hand to it. I nodded, not having had breakfast yet, and the medical staff down in the sub-basements here were coming to the conclusion that my body needed almost twice the normal caloric intake a normal Elf required.

We each took a Bavarian cream, leaving the two apple fritters that remained in the box, and he shared, "The thing is, that for the past two decades, the Council believed that all the Elves in Bloc countries had gotten out. But as there were no voting share families in those countries, only Dearmadta, and some families even today remain hidden from the Council for various reasons." He looked at me pointedly.

"Touche,"

"Just so. And so we had no records of numbers, names, or any way of determining the population of Elves in those hostile environments. Nevertheless, we were convinced all had fled as refugees to more Elf-friendly nations since there were no more public displays of Sapien on Elf violence by their governments after the ultimatum deadline passed. And the Bloc tightened its laws to make it a capital crime to aid in bringing Elves into their sovereign territories. And it applied to anyone aiding 'criminal Elves' in their territories."

I nodded, it was reasonable to believe that anyone who wanted out, got out during that time.

He was starting to nod with me, then his nod turned into shaking instead as he said plainly, "We were wrong."

This had me blinking, and he explained, "The fugitive alert sent to the US government yesterday indicates that there are still Elves trapped in the Bloc countries twenty years later. The Ethiopian Intelligence Agency received a tip that a wanted fugitive, Diedre James, was heading to New York City, and they have demanded she be apprehended and extradited with all due haste."

My mind was working in overdrive, trying to piece together why the Elf Council would be involved in the apprehension of the woman. I was about to ask if she was Elf, but pursed my lips instead, since if she were, then the Ethiopian government would have to have made the request formally to the Council, not the US government.

The smirking lawyer could see me working through it and I narrowed my eyes at his smirk, realizing, "You're withholding a key piece of information Mr. Funnyman. So why is the International Elf Council involved with the apprehension of a Sapien fugitive from an asshole country? And how does it pertain to the conclusion there were still Elves in the Bloc countries?"

"Your instincts are still sharp, Kia. Is it because of your investigative reporter position, or have you always been intuitive?"

"Yes."

It was his turn to say, "Touche," and then he shared the pertinent piece of information I needed to fit into the jigsaw puzzle he was forming, "She's wanted for trial as an Elf sympathizer, and helping to facilitate their escape from Ethiopian territory. And for assault on Ethiopian Military personnel."

"Shit."

"Just so." He shrugged. "The US government had the same reaction, so they are the ones who contacted us since it pertained to Elves due to the nature of the supposed crimes of the fugitive."

I looked at him in horror. "We're not helping to capture her to hand over to the Bloc are we?"

He chuckled. "That's the million-dollar question. But no, if she is championing Elves, we're trying to locate her before the US government does, and we're trying to determine if we can grant her sanctuary or not without breaking any of the covenants of the Accords or international law."

"And can we?"

He shrugged, and shared somberly, "The short answer is... I don't know. That's why the entire law department has been working on no sleep for twenty-four hours trying to come up with something. We have some possible maybes that we'll need to discreetly inquire about with our trusted counterparts in the federal agencies and the US ambassador offices in Ethiopia."

"And if we can't?"

His nonanswer was all the answer I needed, and I found myself unimaginatively repeating myself, at a loss for words. "Shit."

He nodded. "Shit."

He shook his head as if to clear it. "And you're not here for that. You're here for the favor." I grinned and nodded and he rolled his eyes pulling me into an empty office next to the coffee bar and activating the white noise curtain to give us privacy from prying Elvish ears, "It's a bit tricky, but something would make it a lot easier, can you answer me this? Without perpetrating fraud, me knowing what I know about your father."

He was one of the very few people who knew my family's disposition. Me being a Halfling and dad being Sapien. And he asked, "Does your mother own any part of the title to the food truck?"

Not knowing where he was going with it I said, "Well they're married, so she owns half of everything."

"Not the question I asked."

Ok, he was splitting hairs for a reason, so I pulled up all the business documents for dad's business from my secure cloud, and showed him a copy of the title. "Yes, and they put my name on the title too when I became eighteen, thinking I would eventually take over the truck for dad when he gets older and retires."

The man was all smiles. "You too? Ok, this went from being tricky to be the easiest thing. I'll have the motor pool just issue you a diplomatic parking permit that will allow the truck to be parked at any meter, city, or state-owned parking structure without having to pay. And we can save your father yearly licensing fees on the truck... we'll issue diplomatic plates."

I grumped at the man, "I asked if there was anything we could do to get a permit when the city won't issue any new ones, 'without' using Elf privilege. I'm pushing my comfort level on this by asking you for help to begin with."

He shook his head. "This has nothing to do with what you call Elf privilege, Kia, but everything to do with a perk of your job as Senior Council Member. As a Council Member, these are things that come along with the position, like any other job has its own perks. Any of your vehicles that have your name on the title qualify for diplomatic plates."

"Oh." Then my eyes widened. "Oh! Ok, I'm picking up what you're putting down, man. This is great! It will help out our finances so much not having to pay a daily fee to the road pirates."

He chuckled at that. "Always with the colorful descriptives. I'll make the call today, and have the parking permit and plates messengered to your house."

I held up a fist, that he reluctantly bumped, and I told him, "Thanks, Aldrich, I know you don't have time for my family drama, it is much appreciated."

The man waved it off and then prompted, "Agreed upon payment?"

I sighed, looked him up and down critically, then pulled two family discount coupons for dad's food truck from my bag and held them up to the man.

He snatched them out of my fingers before I could change my mind, and I prompted as I absently scratched my left wrist which had been in a cast for so long, "Use them wisely, twenty five percent off one item each is a lot of power and responsibility... those coupons are worth their weight in gold."

Aldrich just winked and nodded with a smug grin, all the lawyers here clamored over dad's cooking whenever I brought some in. "Now if you'll excuse me, I have to go un-fuck this extradition cluster-fuck." He chuckled. "Well, would you look at that, a legal mess that didn't originate with you or your Riicathi Consortium."

I retorted drolly, "Hardy har har," and flipped the man off, causing him to chuckle as he opened the office door and moved back to the hectic mass of legal types. He was good people.

I headed to the private elevators, now I had to figure out what to get Tana for our date tonight. A moment later I was gleeping and backpedaling when the elevator doors opened and I almost ran directly into said girlfriend. I pirouetted around a woman I almost ran over, then tripped over a stack of files someone had stacked next to the wall in their mad rush to find some legal precedence for this 'Elf collaborator'. And did an aerial cartwheel over it to lean against the wall, acting casual like nothing had just happened.

"Umm, Tanny, hi. What are you doing here?" I tucked a strand of hair behind my ear as I looked down.

The look on her face was priceless as she just beamed a smile my way, reaching up to brush her long ebony hair, which she had been growing out for me, back to lay behind her back, revealing the blood-red layer of stubble of the shaved sides. Her near mohawk was almost gone now that the hair was too long for it now. It brought my attention to her graceful neck I longed to nuzzle.

"A little bird told me that you were in the building. I thought you wanted to get together before our date. So I headed on down." She had her come hither look in full force, which made me swallow hard, my favorite parts heating at the sight.

"No you evil woman, you said to keep away until you picked me up. I was just coming for a car and to talk to the solicitors here."

She chuckled in mirth then prompted as she stepped aside, holding the elevator door from closing. "Hmm, too early for lunch... hang out a bit?"

"As tempting as that is, I have some things I need to get done before our date tonight... alone... without a punk rock princess distracting me. But do tell Sonia I finished her latest chapter, and it had me on the edge of my seat. The editors at WTRL said they will messenger it to her today. That girl is a wonder."

She puffed up in pride and agreed, "Yes, she is. And I'll let her know. And she wants another girls' night soon."

"Any time."

Sonia Laun is the sweetest girl you'll ever meet. She is neurodivergent, having the Elf equivalent of Down Syndrome, Kerricyn Syndrome. The Elves push a misleading narrative that they don't get sick, to foster the awe that some people have toward the glamorous Elves that the Council makes sure to show as our public-facing... well, faces. It's all just gaslighting, and I think it will just do more harm than good when people find out Elves are just as flawed as anyone else. I personally think it makes them, us, more relatable to people on the street.

Another negative aspect is that since they are showing this fake front, Evander and Natalia Laun hide their daughter away from the public. As far as I'm aware, she rarely leaves their penthouses here in the Tower. I've only seen her once outside of the building myself.

On my first meeting with her, we had sandwiches, and I learned she wanted to be a writer, something all her tutors and her parents didn't believe she was capable of. I encouraged her and gave her some books and materials on the writing process. And now she is writing the most amazing paranormal urban fantasy book with a main character who is modeled after Tana, which is easy to tell as she idolizes her big sister.

I've been proofreading it and having the editors at the news station go over each chapter for her as a favor to me. They've yet to find anything to mark up, as Sonia compulsively maintains the guidelines of the books of grammar and style she got from me, down to writing footnotes for the editors that highlight which writing rules she followed in each section.

We've had a couple of impromptu slumber parties, though Tana and I are well onto our way to thirty now, you can't say no to Sonia when you see her wide-eyed excitement.

"Great, she'll love that. Sooo, any hints as to what you have to do today, Killy?"

I was all grins as I shook my head. "No, miss nosy. You'll just have to wait and see."

She pouted well, I almost caved and let her know I still had no clue what to get her for Valentine's Day. I didn't want to be cliché with flowers and chocolates.

She looped an arm in mine and made a show of bringing me in a wide berth around the stack of papers I almost scattered down the hall. I'll get her for her amusement at my clumsiness later. "Come along Killy love, I'll walk you down. Cliff will be waiting at the parking garage doors when we get down there.

Her hungry look as the elevator doors closed had me gulping again. And I'm not about to share with you the hot and steamy make-out session we had on the way down.

Chapter 4 – Bazaar

I was in a happy daze a couple of minutes later, when Clifford was driving us out of the underground parking levels in a black luxury sedan. As usual, I sat in the front seat with him instead of in the roomy back seat that resembled a small limousine space.

Swiping his chauffeur's cap from him and jamming it down over my knit cap, I asked, "Question, where does one look for the perfect gift for someone who can just buy an island before lunch?"

He rolled his eyes and tipped the brim of the cap down over my eyes with a finger. "You haven't gotten anything for Valentine's Day for the Aryon yet? You do realize that it's today, right?"

I pulled the cap back up and squinted an eye in mock pain. "Maybe?"

Though he was about my age, he dropped a piece of wisdom on me. "It's usually the ones who have everything that truly have the least... that's what my grandmother shared with me one time."

Then before I could say anything, he added, sounding deep in thought as we pulled out onto the street, "It must get lonely."

I seriously pondered that, and thought about my girl, seeing some of her actions in a new light. I smiled at the man and put his cap back on his head. "You're a genius, man. Yonkers please."

He furrowed his brow, distaste on his face as I looked up the address for our destination since I was positive he wouldn't be familiar with it, I rattled it off for him and he nodded slowly as I shared, "The old Yonkers Power Station."

"The derelict? Hasn't that been torn down?"

I shook my head. "The city planners were debating it, right around the time of the Reveal, but there was a substantial public outcry to preserve it, as its unique architecture makes it a landmark in the borough. A grassroots funding campaign raised enough money from residents to clean up the grounds and inside of the building, bringing it up to safety standards. And one of the biggest flea market swap meets is held inside the main floor of the plant, five days a week."

Then I held my hands out palm up as I explained, "The money raised from the people who pay to have tables there each day pays for the upkeep and for replacing the boarded-up windows, one at a time. And one day they'll have the rest of the funding needed to renovate the entire building."

"The plant's nickname is Hell's Gate, so they call it the Hell's Gate Bazaar," I said.

He balked. "I've heard that name. Isn't it like a cut-rate..." The man trailed off when he caught my raised brow.

I chastised because I knew he was better than that, forgetting Elves have such high standards, "Just because it isn't one of those fancy open-air markets that look like a tourist destination from a brochure, doesn't mean it is some sort of cheap out of the trunk flea market filled with low-income people trying to make ends meet. Well fine, it is, but most of the stuff there is handcrafted or antiques that just need a little TLC to shine. You can find hidden gems there without breaking the bank."

Then to punctuate I added, "My house has more than a few finds my family got there that was within our budget."

I could see him considering my words, then he offered sheepishly, "Sorry, Kia. You're not like any of the other Council Members."

"Thank the Horta for that."

"You realize nobody gets your Star Trek references, Kia. And why thank a rock monster?"

With a smug grin, I pointed out, "You got it, closet geek. And... why not?" Then he deflated when I reached for the radio. Just for that, I found some bubbly pop music to listen to on the way there.

He was checking his mirror more frequently than normal and I cocked my head at him in question, he shared, one eye on the road, one on the rearview mirror, "You've got a whole passel of security today. Something happening I should know about?"

I looked back, to see two black SUVs trailing us by a block. "No, Ivan is helping the security forces to find someone, so my overprotective man mountains have a second car following me until he gets back."

The man sounded patient as he prompted, "That's not fair, and you know it. You almost got killed on their watch, and the Korsivairs see it as their failure. You can't blame them for being so protective now."

Sighing I agreed, "I know, it's just... stifling at times. I feel like I never have any privacy."

"You're a Senior Council Member now, so that ship has sailed."

I flipped him off and he grinned as we headed up past the Botanical Gardens, heading up into Yonkers. And a minute later the old power plant came into view with its smokestacks towering over it. When Cliff saw the packed parking area and at least a hundred people milling about the lot and the front of the building, he winced. "Pietor is going to have a conniption fit. This is a security nightmare."

He pulled right up to the entrance and tried to get out to come open my door but I just opened it and stepped out. He gave me 'the look', and I shrugged my apology. And Pietor pulled up and stepped up to me, another man from the second car running up to slip into the driver's seat to move the car away from blocking other vehicles trying to navigate the lot.

The big man looked first at me, then the building, then Cliff, who shrugged. He opened his mouth but I beat him to it, "It'll be fine, big guy. And hey, I've got you, so nothing is going to happen."

He looked at the people all around us who were just noticing Elves in their midst, then deflated. With a nudge of his chin, Clifford pulled away to find parking somewhere in the maze of cars. Then to me, he rumbled, "Always at my side." I looped my arm in his, it was like arm wrestling a huge tree branch and dragged him toward the doors as people started taking pictures of us on their cells as the murmuring began.

Another capable-looking Elf with a Men in Black vibe stepped wordlessly up to the main doors into the main floor where the bazaar was staged, then just stood there, his mirrored sunglasses hiding his eyes as we stepped inside, people trailing us, whispering about Elves at the swap meet. They had to know we could hear them.

My ears were swiveling everywhere, as I picked up conversations throughout the cavernous space which was filled with tables and booths and hundreds of people bustling about, looking at the wares. It took an effort for me to tune everything out before one of the migraines I got in large crowds started to set in.

It was just a couple of months ago, Grandma and Grandpa Riicathi, who my mother thought were dead, leading Elvish Special Ops away from New York to protect her, had returned in spectacular style, interrupting a meeting of the International Elf Council. They have been teaching me how to ignore all the sounds that come at me by focusing on one thing.

They've also been trying to teach me the martial arts style called Mahta-quárë, a devastating closed-fist combat style thought lost with the Riicathi three hundred years ago when they fled from the Council. But... well, I'm not really a fighter. The one time I tried punching someone, I broke my hand and had to wear the itchiest cast in the world for a few weeks for my trouble.

I'm more of a run away, run away, like brave Sir Robin. And we found my Halfling status with my messed up nervous system didn't lend itself to fighting, though we found I was adept at grappling, which is the opposite of running away... so I saw no practical application for it, other than it was a good exercise since the Cookie Twins discouraged me from jogging in my neighborhood anymore.

So I did what they suggested and found one sound to concentrate on to the exclusion of all else and the sound pressure went down as it all sort of slid into background noise behind my heartbeat.

Pietor grumbled to me, "This is a logistical and security nightmare."

I shook my head and corrected him, "This, is a treasure hunt."

He scanned the various tables near the door and said so low only Elf ears could pick it up, "This... is junk. I can suggest other markets much more suitable, and secure, to peruse, Miss Kia."

With a smirk, I shook my head and assured him as I looked at the... well the junk at the front tables. It was the sort of stuff people rummage from abandoned houses and the ilk and did a cursory job of cleaning and making semi-presentable, but, "One man's trash is another man's treasure, big guy. And besides, the good stuff is near the back, by the heaters and restrooms. There are antiques, furniture, wood-crafts, artist booths, and even painters back there. Some are pretty cringe, but some are gems just waiting to be picked. And the prices aren't astronomical like in the types of markets you're alluding to."

He furrowed his brows as he swept one of his big arms to move back a man trying to get a selfie with me without asking, "And you are looking for something for the Aryon for Valentine's Day... here?"

I nodded as I picked up what looked to be an old chrome hubcap that was fitted with a mirror inside, from a table. It was pretty clever, as the hubcap resembled some sort of rough, art-deco starburst frame. I put it back down and shared, "My family got a lot of our stuff here, and places like this. Though this is the first time I've been here since I Elfed... and there were never so many people gawking at me then."

My cell buzzed and I took it out to look, then snorted. I showed Pietor the screen. Lisa had sent a text, "The socials are buzzing with posts and pictures of you at Hell's Gate. You're shopping without me?"

I sent back, "You're with your man... it's V-day woman."

"I guess there's that. I'll need pictures so I can shop vicariously through you."

"You're so weird, tell me again why Junior and I put up with you?" Junior was our imaginary child since everyone, including Tana, calls Lis my work wife.

"Because I'm awesome, and you love me."

"Against my better judgment. Now shoo, Issac is waiting. Love ya."

"Love you too, Kia."

Then I spent the next forty-five minutes at various booths and tables that had antique or reclaimed furniture, some meticulously restored, some looking one step short of kindling. And every once in a while, some were painted artistically by one of the back alley artisans in charming pastels and florals.

People had started losing interest in the novelty of two Elves wandering through the Bazaar where none have ever ventured before, so we were given a bit of pseudo-privacy in the crowd.

I had all but given up, not finding what I was envisioning, but just as I was turning to tell Pietor that this was a bust when something caught my eye in the back of a stall with a few free-standing full-length mirrors that had tole painting designs painted on the old wooden frames and stand.

The young woman of middle eastern descent, who was possibly nineteen or twenty, had just been staring at us, wide-eyed, a paintbrush in one hand and paint on one cheek. She had stopped her latest project, painting a sunflower field on an old tin watering can. I asked, "Is it ok if I get a closer look at that piece behind the others there?"

She blinked rapidly then looked back at her offerings then at me then back again. "Oh, that? I've had that here for months now and nobody has shown interest. You're Killishia Renner. Your eyes look just like on WTRL... I watch your Killishia's Musings segment religiously."

My cheeks and neck heated as I rubbed the back of my neck as I squinted an eye, "Yeaahh... that's me."

It was a little refreshing to have someone know me from my segment on the news rather than all the social media memes I'm the frequent target of. Then I nudged my chin, she turned back to her. "Oh, yes, of course, Miss Renner. But I have some better items upfront here, it isn't my best work."

I absently said, "Kia," as I stepped past the front table of the booth to the mirrors, then moved one carefully aside to see the item of interest. I whispered, "This is it. It's perfect."

Pietor was looking at it then me in confusion. "This? For the Aryon? For Valentine's Day?"

I was nodding like a loon and telling the man, "You don't understand the symbolism. But yes." Then to the woman I prompted, "I'm sorry, I didn't get your name."

"Pashka."

What a pretty name. "Pashka, how much for this?"

She was smiling as she put her brush down and wiped her hands nervously on the apron with hundreds of colors of paint on it. "I was asking a hundred, but as I said, it's not very popular with..."

"I'll take it." A hundred was almost double what I was hoping to spend, as it would put a dent in my bank balance, but Tanaliashia Laun was worth every penny, and it was perfect for my girl.

I asked, "Do you take debit cards?"

She excitedly nodded and pointed at the little sign on the table that said she accepted cash, debit, and credit cards. Duh, Kia, pay attention. I handed her my card and she used a LaunPay credit card puck that was Bluetooth enabled, then had me enter my pin on her cell.

My cell pinged with the receipt. Then I stared at my purchase then stuck my tongue out to the side as I thought about logistics. "Umm, Pietor, can this fit in the SUV? It won't fit in the trunk of the town car. Or, maybe if we take the mirror off?"

He sighed heavily, like every man on a shopping expedition with women, and just reached out and picked it up like it weighed nothing. I'm sure it was only thirty pounds or so, but still. I informed him, "You look very... domestic there." He sighed again.

I told the vendor as I shook her hand in both of mine, "Thank you so much, Pashka. This is going to make my girlfriend very happy."

"It was my pleasure, um, Kia." Then she took a half step as if to ask something but then stopped.

"What is it?"

She sheepishly held up her cell. I chuckled and said, "Sure."

Then we posed and she took a selfie, she looked overjoyed as she started texting someone, "My sister is going to be so jealous and wouldn't believe me, this is my evidence." She shared a cheesy grin with me. I often wondered what it would be like to have siblings. Since my mom and I both almost died in childbirth, the only child I was destined to be.

Then we said our goodbyes and started to make our way out. Just one table down at an intersection, I glanced at the short hall at the back of the space. I put a hand on Pietor's arm. "Hang tight, big guy, I have to use the girl's room."

"Miss Kia, it isn't..."

"Just stay right here. It's right there, you can see the door and I've been peeing most of my life without incident. I'll be right out."

He huffed in exasperation, "Fine. Ivan owes me for abandoning me with the most stubborn, reckless..."

I stopped him from reciting a million adjectives in two languages, "Love you too. Be back in a flash." And I almost skipped off down the hall. I passed the two doors in the man's room, one to enter and one to exit, and I slipped into the woman's room door at the end of the hall at a cross corridor, the exit was kitty-corner to the entrance.

Then I just grinned at how lucky I was to find the perfect gift for Tana. At least I hoped she would get the symbology of it.

I did my business and washed my hands, glancing in the mirror, only then realizing I had my knit cap on the whole time we were shopping. Can I be any more awkward? Wait, I'll not entertain that thought else something in the cosmos might answer.

Then I slipped out the door and almost immediately stopped before I could step around the corner back into the hall I came from when that feeling of eyes on me returned. I looked back to see a person, in a black hoodie, disappear through the emergency exit door. They were either a woman or a slight man with long brunette hair since some of it escaped the shadowed hood as they turned to the door.

Damn it. I ran down the corridor to the exit and saw the latch had been taped so it wouldn't latch then I looked to see the person moving quickly down the back of the building, hands stuffed in their pockets. I called out as I started after them. "Wait, stop. Why are you following me?"

After a slight stumble, I started to sprint, my blood pumping and adrenaline flooding my system as the world started to blur as I gained on them, even though they were moving faster than any Sapien I knew. They had to be Elf! But that weird speed I got when my body could keep up with my nervous system when the adrenaline was pumping kicked in and I overtook them in a couple of seconds before they could get to the corner of the building.

I really don't know what I was thinking, but I reached out and grabbed their arm. "Wait, I just want to talk!"

And as they turned and I got a glimpse at a feminine face, with muted, crystal blue eyes, and rounded ears, someone came out of nowhere to grab my arm that was holding her as she slid into a familiar fighting stance. The newcomer called out in the voice of a rage-filled teenage boy, "Let go of my mom!"

And I released her to push his arm off mine, but he moved with lightning-fast reflexes, and we exchanged a rapid-fire set of grapples and releases... at my speed. He had faster than Elf reflexes too. What the hell?

And I heard a familiar sound that was so slight I almost missed it. The same sound I heard every time Grams Riicathi's feet made when she moved to attack me in sparring, where I would usually squeak in terror and cringe, much to her chagrin. This woman was using Mahta-quárë! I spun and ducked, snagging the boy's sleeve and twisting him between me and the woman. They collided and she smoothly pulled him behind her, asking, "Jacob! What are you doing here? Stay behind me!"

I held my hands up and then gasped when I got a look at the boy. He had one crystal blue eye like all Elves and one sparkling brown eye. And his mostly Sapien-looking ears had a little point to them. I dropped my hands and whispered to myself in disbelief as his eye dulled and those little points receded to rounded ears as he reversed his manifest, "A... Halfling?"

Both of them were staring at me as if they had just seen a ghost, then Jacob said in a tone that mirrored my disbelief, "Look, mom, it's true, mom, she's like me."

Fut, the actual wuck?

Chapter 5 – Fugitive

We all stood there for a few heartbeats, all of us stunned. Then my eyes widened even further when I put it all together, looking at the woman who was repressing her Elvish traits as mom did. I gasped out, "You're the fugitive from Ethiopia that everyone is looking for. They all think you're a Sapien Elf sympathizer."

She hesitated, looking back toward the corner of the building, her hand tightening on her son behind her. Then she carefully voiced in a distinctly British accent like his, "Is it true, are you really Riicathi? Working with the Council? We aren't the last?"

Aren't the... last? I covered my mouth at the implication. "You're... Riicathi?" When they didn't answer, I prompted, "Yes, the Riicathi now have a seat on the Council. They are trying to make amends for all they put my ancestors through."

She pulled her hood down carefully, revealing a woman around my mother's age, with long brunette hair. Cautious hope sparked in her eyes as they brightened to the familiar crystal blue of Elves as her ears lengthened into sweeping points. Then just as quickly, they rounded again as her eyes dulled. I gasped at the truth of it, only the Riicathi clan could control the amount of Protoelastin in our bodies to manifest back and forth at will. If any other Elf repressed their traits, it would take weeks or months before they could re-manifest. I've been practicing, but still haven't mastered it as her son has.

My family wasn't the last...

With a slight tremor in her tone, she asked, "So Romulus' side of the family yet thrives? The Riicathi are truly free?" Then she licked her lips, deciding as she pulled her hood back up and stood taller and asked firmly, "I formally request sanctuary for myself and my children."

"Children? There are more?"

She looked to be deciding whether to bolt or not as she nodded slowly. "My son and two daughters. When the Ethiopian death squads started hunting, we fled to America on a ship in hopes the rumors of the re-emergence of the Riicathi here were true. And in the Council no less."

I looked past her to the defiant teen, who looked possibly seventeen or eighteen, with his unique heterochromia iridium, giving him two different eye colors, and asked, "And are your daughters... um, like me... Halflings too?"

She shook her head slowly and Jacob snapped out like he was defending them, "No, they're full Elf. They're hiding."

"Jacob!" Then she looked at me intently.

Oh... I sputtered out, "Of course. The Council has been looking for you to try to figure out how to shield you from the Ethiopian authorities. We all believed you to be Sapien. I don't know if this changes things, you being Aelftus. The legal team will have to change their plans."

She narrowed her eyes. "You are not going to hand us over to the Council. They have dogged me my entire life."

I understood her hesitation, my family believed the modern Council's black ops were hunting them as well when in reality, the Launs and Havashires were trying to make amends for the oppression of our clan who were treated like servants to the other voting families and had the grisly duty of being their enforcers and assassins.

Looking back to the door we exited from I told her, "You have my word that you will receive sanctuary... the Council isn't what you think anymore. I don't know if they can shield you yet, but I know who can." I shared a secret I have withheld from the Council myself. "My grandparents on my father's side have a safe house in the city. We can hide you there until the legal department can formulate a plan to shield you from extradition."

I looked back yet again, Pietor would be getting worried about me now, I've been gone a long time. So I told her, "My security will be looking for me any moment. Let me call him before he calls in reinforcements, and we can get your family to the safe house."

She sneered. "The Korsivairs? They're Special Ops. We thought them to be your handlers. They've been hunting us until recently. This was a mistake, you're not handing us over to them."

I held up my hands in a placating manner. "No. I give you my word, they can be trusted. Nobody will hold you against your will. But I can't get you to safety without him calling in backup. Let me call him and we can get you all to safety."

Then I added, "You're family, and Grams and Gramps Riicathi would make anyone who threatens you wish they never heard the name Riicathi."

She looked back at her son, he was shaking his head. "No, mom, you can't trust her." Then she looked back to me and nodded once, cautiously, "Ok. But at the first sign of betrayal, we'll be gone before you know we left."

Nodding, I pulled out my cell and squinted an eye in pain as I dialed. On the first ring, Pietor answered, urgency and a promise of pain to anyone threatening me in his tone, "Miss Kia, where are you?"

"Umm, hi Pietor. I'm fine. I just, umm, have a little problem that only you and Ivan can help me with. But only you two, the others can't know until I can speak with the Council."

I could hear the threat of any danger I might be in his voice, "Miss Kia, what is it? Where are you?"

"Promise first, Big guy."

He huffed in exasperation, "Fine. Now, where are you?"

"I'm behind the power plant. I'm with some people that need my help. I'll wait right here. And again, I'm in no danger, so no Hulk smash, got it?" Then I snerked as I looked at the woman who knew the deadly fighting style of my clan. "Though I'd think you'd be hard-pressed if you tried." The Korsivairs weren't a match for my grandparents, and they were learning the art of Mahta-quárë from them.

"Da, stay where you are, I'm on my way."

Moments later, he was bursting out the exit door, weapon in the ready position, the woman pulling Jacob tighter behind her. When the man mountain saw me standing there under no threat, he hesitated as I widened my eyes at his gun and nudged them down. He looked at it then holstered it and strode up to us, a chastising look on his face.

Aw man, not another lecture. I liked it better when he didn't talk so much.

I told him, "Pietor Korsivair, this is Jacob and his mother..." I trailed off, trying to remember the name Aldrich share with me. "Diedre James." Then I corrected as I gave him a warning look, "Diedre Riicathi."

It looked almost like his hairline swallowed his light brows his eyes widened so far, whether it was because this was the fugitive Ivan was off looking for, or that I just shared she was of my kin. Then I added, "I promised to protect them, give them sanctuary until the Council finds a way to keep her and her family from being extradited. I need to get them someplace safe, to... umm to..."

"Da, to the Renner safe-house."

I blinked dumbly. "You know about that?"

He chuckled. "We suspected, it explained a lot, and there were large amounts of times you spent there where we could not hear you, and their home doesn't have white noise generators as far as anyone knows."

"And you never said anything?"

"Nyet, if you didn't share with us, it wasn't our place to pry into your secrets. You are our charge to protect, and your private life and family is just that, private."

For some reason, that made me relax, a weight taken off of me just like when I finally shared with Tana and Lisa when we got back from Bangkok. I really hated having secrets from the people I care for. And yes, I care for the Cookie Twins too, seeing them as overprotective big brothers.

I noted his eyes on the boy, and he started, "Is he..."

Nodding I said cautiously, "Yes. Like me."

He exhaled long and hard. Then took in the area and said, "Ok, get inside with them. I'll have the car brought around back to load your purchase then send the rest of the detail away. Ivan is already on the way now, I sent the emergency code before I came out here."

I nodded and looked at Diedre. She hesitated, sizing up Pietor as he held a hand out toward the door we left from. She pulled her son beside her and nodded once, and Jacob blurted, "But mom, he's a Korsivair, they were the ones who hunted you and grandpa."

The big man hesitated then told them, "Nyet. We were tasked by the Senior Council Members, the Launs and Havashires, to investigate all suspected sightings of any surviving Riicathi. Not to bring you in, but to extend an overture of peace... to offer recompense for how the Council had used your kin for all those centuries before the Riicathi fled."

They both just stared at him, distrust shadowing their faces. He added in a tone colored with sad regret, "Whenever any teams got close at any of the reported Riicathi sightings, none ever returned unharmed. There were many casualties and many deaths. But by the time others arrived to assist, the suspected Riicathi would always vanish again, to pop up years later in various countries across the globe."

He seemed reticent to share, he seemed almost shamed as he provided, "Ivan and I were on one of the recovery teams in Burma. We never saw them coming. Ivan lasted longer than the rest of the team did, but he never got a look at them, it was after we failed to relay the Council's olive branch that we were pulled out of Special Ops to instead safeguard Senior Council Members."

I hadn't known that. So I was basically... punishment for their failure to bring in my family?

Diedre nodded slowly as she started to pull her son along toward the door. "That was my father. He remembers you Korsivairs. He said you put up a fierce fight."

Jacob pulled from his mother and stood directly in front of Pietor, standing tall, only to the big man's chest, and raising his chin. I tried not to grin and failed. The gargantuan, virtually albino Russian, out massed and out-muscled him by at least twice. The kid had guts, but he was sorely outmatched, since I already saw what he could do, and he didn't know Mahta-quárë, the only thing that would give him a chance.

Diedre snapped, "Jacob." The boy swallowed, losing some of his bravado as Pietor just kept eye contact with him, then he moved beside his mother again in a huff. She scolded him, "What is wrong with you? Do not make challenges you cannot back up. That man would dismantle you without a thought. You aren't a fighter like your sisters."

The boy looked frustrated, then they moved inside with me as I shot a glance up at my protector. Did he look conflicted and... sad?

Inside both Deidre and Pietor's eyes swept around, clearing the area, displaying their keen situational awareness, something I lacked. Then he was on his radio instead of his earbud. I understood why, to demonstrate he wasn't setting them up. Which was technically unnecessary since our Elf hearing would be able to pick up the other side of the exchange on his earbud anyway. It was a show of good faith. "Team two, bring the car behind the power plant for loading, then bug out. We are retiring to the Tower. Confirm?"

"Copy that Alpha, unit inbound, ETA thirty seconds."

Then we waited for my purchase, and my curiosity was killing me. "Jacob, do you have Elf hearing as well? The doctors were curious about me, since I have most of the Elvish traits, just on the low end of the spectrum." Then I quickly added as I winced at my directness, "I'm sorry. I just thought I'd never meet another Halfling."

He seemed to be measuring me up before he slowly nodded and said, "It isn't as good as mom's or my sisters'. I only partially manifested, not fully like you." He indicated my ears offhandedly.

I grinned and squinted one eye as I tilted my head. "Well, about that. These ear shields aren't mine, well they are now, but..." I reached up to slide one of the silver, fur-lined ear shields with its lacy silver tinkling chains which provided a sound barrier to drown out the sharpest of noises of everyday life and exposed my half-length Elf ears.

He blinked and smiled then his mother said, "Oh my, they're adorable."

Gah! Cthulhu preserve me. Why does every Elf use the A word like that? My cheeks burned in embarrassment as my ears swiveled toward the sound of someone dropping something in the main room at the bazaar, which was heard above all the sounds of people talking and moving about the space. Then I placed the ear shield back on.

His smile faded as he grumped like the teen he was, "Her's even articulate." His didn't? Then again, they had looked mostly Sapien, a little pointed at the tips when he was manifested.

We heard, "Unit in position, bugging out," over the big guy's coms, and he replied, "Copy. Thank you for your assistance today, gentlemen. Alpha out."

"Copy that, it was our pleasure. Team two out."

Then when the boy started toward the door, I placed a hand on his arm and shook my head. "Not yet, wait for Pietor to say when." Diedre inclined her head to her son and he stopped moving, looking perturbed.

We heard a second vehicle pull up, then a car door and the vehicle proceeded to pull away and drive off. Diedre, Pietor, and my ears were all slowly tracking it until it turned the corner of the building. My bodyguard lifted my purchase and then backed out the door, looking around before saying, "Come." We all slipped out and I opened the door for them and they slipped in, and slumped in the back seat, Diedre pulling her hood farther down to hide her face, and with a prompt from her, Jacob pulled up his hood while Pietor loaded the trunk.

I debated on whether to sit in the back with them or to ride shotgun and was about to ask what would make them feel more comfortable when the decision was taken out of my hands when Ivan opened the passenger door and folded into the SUV's front seat. Where in Great Caesar's Ghost did he come from? I hadn't heard his approach in the slightest, and how did he get here so fast?

He didn't even look back at us, instead, staring out the windshield as I slid into the back-facing third-row seating across from Diedre and Jacob in the large vehicle. "Miss Kia, what chaos rides on your heels today?"

"Ha ha, Mr. Funnyman. I liked it better when you guys didn't talk much." He pulled down the sun visor on his side of the car and watched me in the little mirror in it as I slid in beside, well beside my newly found family members. He had a cheesy grin on his face and I sighed, "But thank you for coming. How did you get here so fast?"

He said as Pietor closed the trunk and then joined him in the front, "Special Ops were tracking the James woman, but lost her a couple of miles south of here."

Now it was my turn to grin like a penguin who found the perfect pebble, "Ivan Korsivair, I'd like you to meet Diedre and Jacob James... or Riicathi as the case may be. They're Aelftus, not Sapien."

This finally had him twisting in his seat, eyes wide in surprised shock, indecision painting his expression as a thousand things appeared to flash through his mind. He repeated, "Riicathi?" He was likely wondering if he should be calling in a protective detail or not.

Pietor simply said, "We're bringing them to the Renners."

Ivan nodded slowly. "Da, the safe-house." Did everyone know about Grams and Gramps Renner?

Diedre voiced it, "Is this safe-house known to all? To the... Council?"

"Nyet. But we..." he swung a finger between his brother and himself, "...believe it to be some sort of underground shelter for families who do not wish the Council to know their location, families who haven't come out as Elves after the Reveal."

I had to know as I shook my head in disbelief. "You two got all of that just because you couldn't hear us in the house at times?"

"Da. That and now that we know who your mother is. We assume the Renners hid your grandparents and mother from us there, and your grandparents led us off to South America, leaving her behind at the safe house." Ok, they weren't just a couple of pretty faces, my boys had big brains to go with their big biceps.

Diedre typed something on her cellphone as she studied me for the tenth time as we traveled in awkward silence even though I had a septillion questions and I'm sure they did as well, but they seemed quite reticent to speak around the Cookie Twins. Then her cell buzzed a couple of miles later and she glanced at it. Then she said, "Korsivair, pull over at the end of the block."

Pietor just eyed her in the rearview mirror, eyes narrowed at the demand. Then pulled over to the curb. Then two shadows dropped on either side of the SUV from somewhere, almost soundlessly, the back doors swung open and two women in oversize hoodies slipped into the back on either side of me.

I lamely... ducked for some unfathomable reason, don't try to make sense of it, it's just my quirky flight or flight reflex, as I've said, I don't have a fight reflex. And Elf fast, Ivan had his sidearm drawn and swinging back toward the newcomers, but Diedre was straddling me in the same instant, and in a movement, I almost couldn't follow, she had him disarmed and Ivan's gun pointing at Pietor who had his gun three quarters drawn.

I squeaked out, "Everyone, stop!" And looked at everyone.
Diedre was looking down at her chest, where Ivan had a wicked-
looking military knife an inch from her breastbone. She cocked
an eyebrow and said in an almost academic tone, "You've
improved since you faced father, Korsivair."

I was still covering my head as I looked from side to side at
the two newcomers who had tiny stiletto blades drawn and one
each pointed toward the boys, then to Jacob, who looked just as
stunned as me. Then Diedre engaged the safety, dropped her grip
on the gun, letting it swing freely by the trigger guard, telling
Ivan as she offered it to him. "Poor choice of sidearm, the safety
is a hindrance and costs you in your reaction time." Then she
said as the newcomers lowered their blades, "My daughters,
Charity, and Mercy."

They pulled their hoods back, to reveal two women around
my age who looked identical to each other, twins, and looked like
younger versions of Diedre herself. Ivan lowered his knife as he
accepted the gun, cleared it, then re-holstered it as Pietor re-
holstered his own. He growled, "That was reckless, you should
have informed us we would be joined by others." Then he added
in his defense, "I would have armed differently if I had known
Riicathi were involved."

I looked from side to side, Diedre still straddling me, and
offered a hand lamely to the woman on my right, "Umm... hello,

Mercy, I'm... umm, your cousin, Killishia, I guess?" She looked to be twitchy from all the adrenaline as she stared at my hand before tentatively shaking it.

As the car started moving again, Diedre sat back down with Jacob as Ivan seemed to nod to himself. "They were the decoys we were trying to locate while you watched Kia at the Bazaar, clever."

They all looked smug as I turned to the other woman. "Charity." As I started to offer my hand, she held out a fist to bump. Immediately I was feeling like a fool as I shook her fist. I closed my eyes, how awkward can I be?

Charity seemed nonplussed as she cocked her head at me, looking into my eyes and turning to her little brother. I don't know why I was expecting the daughters Diedre spoke of to be children. She said as she looked back and forth, "It's true then, mother? She is Riicathi... and..." She looked to the front seat cautiously and offered, "Like Jake?"

As the woman started to nod and open her mouth, I blurted, "Yes, I'm Riicathi, and the boys here know I'm Halfling, though most of the Council and the general public don't... the Launs and Havashires think it could cause a panic if people knew we were possible."

A portion of my mind was oddly relieved, knowing that now the Riicathi line would not die out with me as I looked around at Diedre's children.

I pulled out my cell and made a quick call. "Grams? Hi. Yes, happy Valentine's Day. No no, Grams, listen. I'm bringing in a family that needs your special kind of help. Yes. Ok. We'll be there in about a half hour. I'm calling mom now."

Chapter 6 – Safe House

Here we are now, an hour and a half later, waiting for dad who shut down the food truck early to come meet us here at his parents' house, as I listened to the surreal reunion of what I have learned are two branches of the Riicathi family.

Gramps was not amused when we showed up with the Cookie Twins. I had to assure him after giving him a big hug once we went inside, the boys standing guard outside, as the rest of us entered the basement via the hidden staircase and into the safe house portion of the Renner's, "They already knew, they figured it out themselves simply because there were times they couldn't hear us inside while they were guarding me."

He looked at the door, double-checked the sound curtain was active, then huffed out a chuckle, "And we refused the Council's offer to install white noise curtains in the house here for privacy. Clever boys."

They grinned as I made the introductions in the living room that was a mirror image of the one upstairs... the entire basement being a replica of the upper living space so that people seeking refuge didn't feel like they were stashed in some dank and dingy basement. Then I asked, "Are Grams and Gramps Riicathi here?"

I gleeped and spun, crouching slightly with a hand up in an improvised Karate chop when Grams Riicathi stepped out of a

shadowed corner of the living room. Nobody else except Jacob
seemed surprised. Then I blurted out a startled, "Gah!" when
Gramps Riicathi laid a hand gently on my shoulder.

I stumbled, my foot catching on the edge of the throw rug, and
pitched forward. Before I could make my recovery, Gramps
caught me by the waist and I dangled an inch off the floor as he
smiled lovingly at me and placed me gently in front of him.

As my cheeks heated, I hugged the man. "I had it, Grandpa."

"Of course you did, sweetie." He winked at me.

Charity was commenting, "She's as clumsy as you, Jacob... it
must be a Halfling trait."

The boy grumped out, "I'm not clumsy, Char."

Then all the attention turned to Diedre as Grandma Renner
and mom came out of the kitchen where the smells of Grams'
scintillating cooking was coming from, wiping their hands on the
aprons they wore. And I made the introductions all around,
realizing I'd be doing it all again once dad arrived.

And here we were now eating a mouth-watering
Mediterranean meal that only Grams Renner and dad can cook...
him getting his culinary wizardry from his adoptive mother, while
Diedre regaled us of the plight of their side of the family.
Everyone had missed lunch with the eventful morning, so Grams
insisted on cooking a late lunch for us.

Diedre asked the elder Riicathis who looked to be fit forty-somethings when they were both over one hundred; mind-boggling to me when I thought I was Sapien and that would have been mid-life to me, but the Aleftus can live up to three hundred, "You're familiar with your grandparent's story?"

They nodded, but when she saw me shaking my head, she went on for my benefit, "When the Council's forces had virtually wiped out our clan, forcing them to do the Council's bidding one last time, dispatching a young family and their Halfling baby to keep the Aleftus hidden from the roundies." She paused and looked at dad. "No offense, Cyrus." He inclined his head, looking amused, and she went on, "They led the remains of our clan in an exodus to the New World, with its vast lands the Riicathi could hide in, free of the Council's draconian rule over them."

She looked pained as she related the tragic history, "Seven... that was all that remained of our people. Led by the twins, like my daughters, Romulus and Remus created a safe haven for the Riicathi, finding other Elves who had fled to the New World and creating a thriving community."

She studied the food on her fork as she reflected upon the tale. "By the end of the century, the Riicathi were thriving as well, adding almost two dozen to our numbers. But the unthinkable happened, the Elf Council realized the unrestrained bounty the

Americas had to offer and set up a presence there. Bringing in forces to repatriate any Elves there and populate the growing regions of the States."

She tapped her fork on the edge of her plate. "When they attempted to pacify the community the Riicathi built, not knowing their identity, they came in force, and lost sixty men before realizing who they were facing, five Riicath gave their lives that the brothers could escape with the rest of the clan and the other Elf families they protected."

She took a bite, making a sour face over the words she shared, "When ship after ship arrived over the next few years, with more and more Council security forces aboard, they hunted the 'Riicathi Rebels'. Though the security forces were routed again and again, their numbers kept increasing, and the brothers knew it was just a matter of time before they would be overwhelmed. So they determined it was time to flee this new land that they had made their own, or the Riicathi may finally be ended."

Mercy took up the narrative when her mother seemed to be lost in thought, "They decided to split up to go to opposite sides of the globe, to give the Riicathi a better chance for survival from the relentless Council."

Charity smiled and said in amusement, "The compound was raided as the plans were made, and Romulus and his group held off the attackers while calling out to Remus to flee with the others. All thought Romulus and his line fell to the Council all these years until a few months back when word reached us that the Riicathi had miraculously resurfaced in New York City, and they were again under the Council's control."

Diedre looked to have gotten her wits about her again, looking truly amused as she shared, "We were planning to run a rescue mission after we got the last of the Elves out of Ethiopia. But our network of informants was sharing confusing news. That these other Riicathi weren't the servants of the Elf Council, and that the child who led them was a disruptive voice in the Council... being among their number."

Chuckling she twirled her fork toward me. "We discounted what they shared since we know how the Council operated, they saw us as a blunt tool to be used. And the rumors were that this young Riicathi had impossible green eyes?" She looked at her son and shook her head slowly. "There would be no way they would allow one of those they actively killed in the past to be one of their numbers."

Then she shrugged as Charity opened her hands, palm up toward me. "And then we saw the pictures. A blended. A Halfling like Jake. And if that were true, was the rest as well?"

Diedre smiled at her children. "And here we are, in need of help... from family, and hoping all we heard was true."

I prompted, "So you've been in Ethiopia all this time?" I thought that was suspect because the kids all had a British accent when their mother did not.

The woman chuckled. "No, I was raised in Charlotte Amalie by my father, and..."

I interrupted. "The Virgin Islands?" That explained her lack of accent. Mom cocked a brow at me for my rudeness, I lowered my head in embarrassment, "Sorry, go on."

Deidre chuckled. "When I was fourteen, one of the Whisperers informed us that witnesses have seen Elvish Special Ops starting to scour all U.S. Atlantic Island Territories, on intel of a Riicathi sighting. We don't know who gave us up, but we packed up that day and moved halfway around the globe to Cape Town." She grinned and shared because of my last outburst, "Yes, Africa."

I squeaked, stopping myself from interrupting again, but she cocked her head, "What is it?"

In a small voice, I asked, "Whisperers?"

She chuckled again, I'm glad I was amusing someone other than Lis and Tanny, then she shared, "Like the Renners here, the network of underground helpers for Elves in need. They have their eyes and ears everywhere."

Oh. That just brought up a septillion other questions but I kept my trap shut, and felt a little pride for my grandparents.

When I first found they had been running an Elf safe-house, I was proud of them then, but now to learn they were part of a network of sanctuaries and watchers? Too cool and James Bond of them.

She seemed a little melancholy. "I met my husband there, from a non-voting clan, the Davies, six years later, we were married the following year. What a whirlwind romance that was." She closed her eyes and shimmied her shoulders in memory, a gentle smile ghosting her lips. "He died in a fishing boat accident near Madagascar two years later. And I didn't even get a chance to mourn when word reached us of a Special Ops team converging on our home had us fleeing to Burma or Myanmar."

She stood and started pacing. "The team tracking us was good, real good, and got closer than most. They arrived in Burma directly after us, they were led by the Korsivairs out there," she nudged her chin in the direction of the street. "Dad put me on a seaplane then went to face the ten-man team alone. I thought I'd never see him again, as I was whisked away by the Whisperers to the Falkland Islands."

Diedre was animated and aggravated as she tied her hair back in a ponytail with an elastic band she had on her wrist. Then she tapped the table with a finger. "But I should have known not to doubt the old man. He showed up two days later, with healing bruises and scrapes, and a nasty black eye, telling me we were safe for now, he left a false trail toward Saudi Arabia before doubling back to meet me."

She smirked. "And it was a week or two later we learned I was pregnant, with the twins. I raised them there, the Council never learning our location, and as time went by, a decade later the ache in my heart which missed my husband lessened its hold just a bit... enough to let in a rapscallion of a Roundie to worm his way into my heart a couple of years after the Reveal. And I showed him my true nature."

Then her smile fell she cooled a little. "Randall wasn't the man I had made him out to be in my heart, because when he learned that I was again pregnant, he was a Sapien and I an Aelftus, the coward ghosted me and the girls, heading back to England."

Then she looked lovingly at her son as we all seemed to be leaning in rapt attention to the story. "And then along came my miracle, my Jacob. It was a difficult delivery with many complications. I flat-lined during the delivery, and the doctors did an emergency C-Section to save my boy while they worked on restarting my heart."

She chuckled and grinned at us. "They were apparently up to the task, and I think that was a sign that I'm done having children now." She reached out to place a hand on Jacob's cheek and rested her other hand on Mercy's shoulder.

That was similar to the trouble mom had with my birth, as they almost lost us both. It must be something about a pregnancy with a Halfling. From what I've gathered, with the limited information I have been able to dig up about the two Halflings and their families that the Council had killed, is that they were the only two known Halflings to survive birth. Others had been stillborn or the mothers and children died in childbirth.

It seems the Riicathi women are made of stouter stuff, for two of them to survive a Halfling birth. Was there something about my kin that made us more able to become pregnant with one and survive? I'd have to ask the doctors on the medical floor in Laun Tower about it one day.

The woman sat back down and tapped her fork idly on the side of her plate again. "Ever since, after I recovered, and my girls were old enough and trained, we have been heading out to hotbeds of Elves in need, where the Whisperers weren't able to lend aid. So when we learned there were still Elf families stranded and in hiding inside some of the Laramer Bloc countries, and the Ethiopian government closing in on a group, we had to go."

She smirked and Charity shared, "That's when everything went all FUBAR. And we find ourselves on the run like mom used to be."

Mercy added, "And the worst part of it all, isn't us being hunted."

I finished for her, already seeing the restrained frustration and rage in her eyes, "It's that there are still Elves trapped there."

They all nodded and Jacob growled, "Mom and my sisters won't let me fight. I could have helped. Now those Elves are..."

Diedre reached over to clasp one of his hands in hers. "You know you haven't completed your martial training yet. Your coordination problem is a detriment." He gave a pained look like that statement had cut him to the quick, and she pulled him to her with one arm and kissed the top of his head, "You're perfect just the way you are, love." He looked just as embarrassed as any other teen with his mother doting over him.

I offered, raising a finger in the air. "Actually, I know a little something about that." All eyes turned to me, Dad standing to move behind mom to rub her shoulders. "Did you see how fast Jacob was moving when we grappled, Diedre?"

She nodded and shared, "He has bursts of speed like that from time to time, I almost can't follow sometimes. But something about being blended, a Halfling, is a detriment to his reflexes."

I grinned and shared what I've learned from Doctor Baahir Ahmed, "It seems that our nervous systems, which are mostly Sapien, can't keep up with the Aclftus quick synapses and neuron firing in our brains. But when we're in high-stress situations, with adrenaline flooding our systems, our bodies can keep up, like our nervous systems are supercharged."

Grandpa Riicathi nodded. "It's true, there have been times Killishia here has moved faster than any Elf I have ever witnessed."

Grams Riicathi chuckled. "The rest of the time I swear the girl has three left feet."

"Graaaams."

"Oh, it's true sweetie. Own it."

"Yes ma'am."

Then Dad prompted, "So you four are the last of Remus' line then? How did you lose your father?"

The woman smirked, truly amused, "I never said we lost him."

Jacob shared, looking at me like he hadn't seen me before this like he was weighing my words about us to see if they were true. "Grandpop is still down in Stanley in the Falklands. He's coordinating the arrival of the Elves mom and my sisters were able to spirit out of Ethiopia. He runs a sanctuary with some of the Whisperers there."

Oh! More Riicathi! I don't think my smile could have grown any bigger at the news. Looking around, everyone else looked just as excited, especially Grams and Gramps Riicathi.

Mom was chuckling, and shared, "You, I like Diedre. You're wicked." The two women shared a borderline unhinged grin. My mom is anything but what you'd call... well, remotely normal. She's so friggin' awesome.

My smile was big before I noted the time. Gack! This was our first Valentine's Day and I was supposed to be meeting Tana in just a couple of hours. I had a feeling that that wasn't going to happen, and my heart fell. I wanted to have the perfect night with her. I glanced at my cell and sighed, it wouldn't work down here with the electronic jammers and white noise curtain my grandparents had running.

I held it up and shared, "I've got to go upstairs. There's a few calls I have to make."

When I got curious looks from almost everyone, I shared, holding up a halting hand to our newfound family members, "The lawyers for the Council, and likely the Launs and Havashires." I forestalled the retort from them. "We have to figure out what the Council can do to shield you, which should be so much easier now that we know you're Aelftus. You should have a lot more rights that are covered by the Accords. And if so, the Senior Members of the Council need to be brought into the loop. I won't tell them where you are until I have assurances you won't be handed over for extradition."

Then I went on, "Aaaand, I have to call a contact at the local police department since the Sapien government has them looking for you too." Then in a forlorn tone I added meekly, "And I have to tell Tanny that we need to postpone our Valentine's Day plans."

It was Jacob that said, wide-eyed, "Sounds like you're connected. The Council and the Police? Cool."

My cheeks heated and Diedre stepped up to me as I turned back to the door. She held her cell up. "I've a call to make too." I nodded and we exited to the stairs, outside of the white noise generators and jamming field. She stayed there and started texting while I went upstairs and slipped out the hidden door under the main staircase.

I flopped down on the overstuffed sofa and took a deep breath and started dialing.

Chapter 7 – Red Tape

Tana joined us thirty minutes later. I ran upstairs and answered the doorbell when Gramps Renner said as he looked at a notification on his LaunWatch, "Someone's at the door, Kia."

I couldn't stop smiling when I swung the door open and she virtually struck a pose for me as she wiggled her brows. I hugged her tight, pulled her inside, and shut the door, "Tana? What are you doing here?"

She shrugged and attempted to look aloof, but she had a little tell when she was bashfully nervous, biting the corner of her lip. "Just wanted to see you and support you on Valentine's Day, even if you did cancel on me, lady." She gave me a hungry look and I heated up all over as I looked down and tucked a strand of hair behind my ear.

"Oh... ok."

She pointed down and I nodded, then she was dragging me to the hidden door I showed her recently. When I was cleared by the security system, I opened the door and we slipped in. She pulled me close as the door closed and the blue light above the door indicated the white noise curtain was still active. My girl leaned in and just brushed my lips with hers as she prompted, "You're terrible at speaking in code. So what is the real reason you had to cancel? I heard the stress in your voice. And I know it wasn't to discuss the differences between Cthulhu and the Great Spaghetti Monster In the Sky with your grandparents. You're such a geek."

I winced in pain over my lame excuse, I was drawing a blank, knowing I shouldn't reveal the fugitive everyone was looking for was here. Then my eyes lingered on her lips hovering bare millimeters from mine, and was about to do something about it when Mom blurted, "Tana! I'm glad you could join in our little family drama."

I closed my eyes tight for a moment, then whined out as we took a step from each other, "Moooom."

We turned and both of us froze, everyone was in the living room replica, all eyes on us. I waved lamely from my waist, "Umm... hi everyone." I pointed toward Tana and shared with Diedre's family, "This is Tanaliashia Laun, daughter of Evander and Marcillia Laun... my girlfriend."

There were some surprised looks, more likely than not because of who she was rather than the fact I was dating another woman. "Tana, this is Diedre, the fugitive everyone is up in arms about in the Tower. And her children, Charity, Mercy, and Jacob."

It was my punk princess' turn to look shocked. Her eyes flicked to their ears then she looked even more surprised. And with years of etiquette and manners drilled into her, she composed herself and said as she inclined her head, "It is a pleasure to meet you all. It's good to know that my trouble magnet here isn't the only one who can keep the Council up in arms."

And as she shook hands with Diedre, I shared, "Oh, and they're Riicathi, like me."

She coughed as she aborted whatever she was about to say and looked at me incredulously. "Way to bury the lead, reporter girl."

I grumped out, "Investigative reporter." Then with a smirk I added, "And if you thought that was the lead. Jacob?"

The boy stepped out from behind his overprotective family, and I didn't even need to voice the true lead for me as she whispered, "Another Halfling? Mom and dad are going to shit bricks."

Everyone sat as I gave a quick overview for her. And she kept glancing at Diedre, who had been staring at her stoically. "What?"

Diedre said in a cold tone. "You're a Laun. One of the main Council families who enslaved mine to do the deplorable work the Council didn't want to dirty their hands with and then hounded us for three centuries. And... the head of our family," she indicated me with a slight lifting of her chin, "Is romantically involved with you? I just can't reconcile that in my head."

"I get that. But like Killy here, I'm my own person. And I personally love the chaotic knots she's been tying the Council in ever since she Elfed." Then she added, "I won't apologize for who I am, and can only offer an apology for what my ancestors put you through. It was unconscionable, and I think that's what keeps father and Natalia Havashire up at night. That's why they've been trying to make reparations the past few decades."

My cousin looked her up and down and shared, "You don't look like your dossier."

"I get that a lot."

Then with a slow, shared nod, they seemed ok with each other after that. Had Diedre been sizing her up? And... "Speaking of the head of the Riccathi. Now that you've resurfaced, Diedre, as my senior, you should really lead after this mess is sorted."

She chuckled, and Jacob's eyes widened in excitement, then she shook her head. "No."

"What do you mean, no?"

"In general, it means negative."

"Smart ass."

She shrugged. "By all accounts and the information your grandparents have shared with me tonight, you are the right person for this, forward-thinking and compassionate, not having the animosity the rest of us harbor since you've only known of your heritage a very short time. And you've created unprecedented turmoil in the Council, and have championed the non-voting clans. If this is what you are capable of in simply two months, what might you accomplish for the Riicathi and all the oppressed Aelftus in the long term?"

Huh. Was that why Grams and Gramps Riicathi simply refuse to even talk about the subject whenever I try to offer them the leadership of our clan?

"Why does everyone think I'm such a disruptive influence?"

Dad said with a chuckle, "Because you are, Itty Bit."

I sighed in exasperation then shared with Tana what I already told the others, "Aldrich and his team of legal hamsters are all running in the wheel to stop Diedre's extradition. He says it made their job so much easier, with a lot less red tape, knowing Diedre is Aelftus, not Sapien. He's going to get back to me on the plan of action once they iron it all out with the provisions in the Accords."

Then I grinned at my girl. "And I informed your parents. I think I shocked them into silence for a few seconds over the fact I was actually keeping them in the loop. Though I haven't shared with anyone over the phone that they are Riicathi since you keep telling me nothing is safe to relay over the phone."

She chuckled and grasped my hand. "And how was the news received?"

I shrugged. "Your mother shared she was going to put more pressure on the legal team, then would have Ivan and Pietor coordinate an extraction with local Police, once they are given the all clear from Aldrich."

She nodded slowly an eye on me in accusation. I huffed out at her jealousy, "Yes, De Luca is in the loop and is put out that I won't share Diedre's location until I'm given the all clear from Aldrich too. And me saying in an official tone, 'Elf Council business', didn't seem to go over very well according to the tirade of creative swearing from her which I hung up on."

When her scrutiny didn't waver, I defended, "Hey, she's the only contact I have with NYPD."

She finally broke into a smile. "Just messin' with ya, Killy."

"I hate you."

"And yet you sleep with..." She trailed off as she remembered my parents were right there. She had the good sense to look embarrassed as mom cocked her head at her, an amused look on her face.

Then we all settled in in the nervous wait, while Diedre shared with us the events that led up to the raid on the safe-house in Ethiopia, and the fight to get out of the country. It sounded that if it weren't for Mercy and Charity, she wouldn't have made it. And the authorities there still don't know how the 'Elf Sympathizer' seemed to be in multiple places at once, and was able to take down so many of their fighters to escape into the night.

After dinner, it was getting late, and mom and dad were talking about retiring back home. And interrupted Jacob and Tanny laughing hard at my attempts to follow Jacob's instruction on how to repress my Elvish traits and reassert them as the rest of the Riicathi could. Tana had tried helping me once before but wasn't able to articulate what I needed to do as clearly as Jake.

They were in the middle of a great laugh as I looked in the mirror, concentrating on breathing out as I let my awareness of my ears and eyes sort of slide out with my breath. My left eye had dulled and my right ear rounded, making me look goofier than a cartoon character who was hit by a falling anvil.

Gah! I let it drop and my Elvish traits reasserted themselves.

Dad informed me, "There's nothing we can do here until word comes in, so your mother and I are going to..."

Grams Renner said as she looked at her LaunWatch, "Ivan is at the door, knocking."

I swallowed. This was it, wasn't it? Dad nudged his chin toward the door, and he led me, with Tana attached to my hand by our laced fingers, out and up to the main floor. Dad opened the door. "Ivan."

The big man started, "Mr. Renner... Cyrus." Then he looked past him to me, "Miss Kia, the legal pool is trying to contact you, they asked me to relay that to you."

I nodded nervously and prompted, "Is it good news?"

"I do not know, as they would not share with me." Then he inclined his head at the three of us and stepped down off the porch to return to his post. "Cyrus, ladies," and dad closed the door.

I looked down at my cell, five unanswered messages now blazed away on it now that I was out of the basement, all from Aldrich. And I tapped to return the call as I started to pace, dad and Tana watching me in anticipation.

Chapter 8 – Asylum

How can things go so sideways? I panted as we slid to a stop to look out of the alley the next day. As we waited for the all-clear from Grams and Gramps Riicathi to proceed to the next alley, I thought back to everything that transpired before what was supposed to be a quick car ride to Laun Tower from the Renner house.

It was only last night that Aldrich had shared with me, that there were provisions for both extradition and asylum laid out in the Reveal Accords, and every nation except the Laramer Bloc countries were signees. So international law would back us if the Council decided to grant asylum to Diedre. Apparently, the Ethiopians didn't know about her children.

"You should be receiving a call any minute, Kia, that the Elf Council is calling an emergency meeting. All Senior Council Members are to assemble in the next hour to vote."

I sighed, and absently scratched at my wrist, the phantom itchiness of the removed cast still persisting. "Thanks for the heads up, Aldrich. And I really appreciate all the work you and your team put into this." Somebody was getting a big fruit basket when all this was over.

I turned to Tana. "You catch all that?" She nodded and I shared with dad, "It looks like the Elf Council will be able to shield Diedre, but I have to get up to Laun Tower, the Council is going to be calling an..." My cell dinged and I saw the expected summons as I finished while holding my cell up, "...emergency vote."

He nodded and said, "Your mother and I can..."

Tana interrupted, "It's ok, Mr. R. I can bring the troublemaker in... or better yet, her security detail, I'll ride with her. I'll have to be there as her Ráquen anyway."

He nodded slowly and reached out to give my shoulder a little squeeze, "Ok, it's settled then. I'm going to bring your mother home, Itty Bit, I need to get some sleep before I have to get up at four AM."

I nodded and he kissed the top of my head and ushered us back downstairs to inform the others. Diedre wanted to come to stand in the Council Chamber as the vote was made, but Grandma Riicathi said, "Absolutely not. Until the vote is complete, there is the very real danger that the police could pick you up without the protection of the Council... and that is assuming the vote is favorable. The Renners have a network that can spirit you from the city if it doesn't go your way."

The woman huffed in exasperation. "Of course, you're right, Audrey." Then she turned to me, her eyes locking on mine, "Inform us the moment the vote is concluded?"

I nodded. "Of course."

Then dad prompted me, "Hold on a moment while we say our goodbyes. Your mother and I will walk you up."

I nodded as he and mother went around to say goodnight to everyone, and hugged Grandma and Grandpa Renner. I added, "Bye Grams, PopPop." And they hugged me too, yay!

Then Tanny and I followed mom and dad up topside, Diedre calling after us, "Godspeed, Killishia."

As soon as we were outside, I put up my thumb toward Ivan in a classic hitchhiking movement. He chuckled and alerted team Charlie that the 'Council Asset' was on the move, and the other teams were to safeguard 'Homeplate'.

I prompted, "Team Charlie?" as he ushered us to the SUV at the curb where Pietor moved to open the back door for us. "Does that mean there's an Alpha and Bravo team out here too?"

"Da, one for your family, and one for the family you brought in as it introduces a layer of danger and uncertainty since multiple groups are searching for them, or the woman at the very least."

"The woman has a name, big guy. Diedre. Is this standard operating procedure or something?"

"Always the reporter... Nyet, nothing about this, or you, is a standard operating procedure as you insist upon putting yourself in danger on a regular basis."

Tana snorted and I gave her an incredulous look after crinkling my nose and squinting fiercely at the big Russian. A swift ride across the river to Manhattan later, with what looked like at least two other vehicles trailing us, we found ourselves at Laun Tower.

Even though it was after hours and the tower was closed to all people but Elves, well except the sub-level train platform, it was bustling with nervous activity. People were rushing about and I recognized quite a few Senior Council Members and their entourages hustling in, and to the private elevator banks. A couple caught sight of me and gave me inscrutable looks. Was it that obvious that I was involved with the reason they were called in for this emergency session? Well fine, I was in a way, but, just, come on.

I squeaked in surprise when someone walked right past us, between Tana and me, and looped arms with us, "Come along, ladies, the Council Chamber awaits." I blinked at Natalia Havashire, one of the two leaders of the Havashire family, the only family with as much power and influence as Tana's.

My girl seemed amused at my surprise and then said to the arm thief, "Hello Aunt Natalia."

"Hello, dear."

Oh, and I learned recently that she was also the twin sister to Tana's dad, Evander Laun. The woman studied me for a moment, then looked around and seemed to bite her tongue, aborting what she was going to say with so many sensitive pointed ears around the space.

She brought us to an elevator and dragged us in, Ivan and Pietor stopping outside on either side of the door and politely stopping others from joining the three of us. When the elevator closed, Natalia placed her palm on the control screen and it scanned her hand, then other controls showed up on the screen than the standard ones. She tapped something and the yellowish light in the ceiling turned a pale blue as a sound curtain draped the elevator car in blessed silence.

The private elevators could do that? I tried to see what else the elevator was capable of but she just smirked at me in mischief and cleared the screen, hitting the button for the Council Chamber level. "Is it true, Killishia?"

I blinked then offered, "That I found Diedre, the fugitive everyone is looking for, or that she's Aelftus?"

She waved that away airily with her hand. "No, that she's Riicathi? We read the subtext of what you were carefully not saying."

I nodded as the elevator started gaining speed on its express trip to near the top of the skyscraper, I was beaming with pride as I shared, "Yes. It seems we can add four more names to the rolls of my clan." Then I looked around lamely as if I were verifying that the three of us were alone there and whispered anyway,

"What I couldn't say over the phone, out in the open, was that Diedre's youngest child... well, he's sort of like me."

She furrowed her brow and Tana added in a normal tone of voice, "He's another Halfling. He can't manifest as fully as Killy here. He has dual colored eyes, one Aelftus blue, the other brown."

Natalia gasped, a hand on her chest. "Another? How are we going to hide this?"

Tanny and I shared a look and I shrugged and said, "Maybe it's time we don't? It seems clear that I'm not just a fluke. If the Riicathi have two, there's bound to be others out there somewhere who survived birth. It seems near-death experiences are common with the difficulties of Halfling births."

She murmured more to herself than us, "The panic a revelation like that may cause..."

It was my girl who backed me, saying to the older Elf, "But think of how much worse it would be down the line if people found out the Aelftus had been hiding this from them. That panic could become something worse."

I shared my thoughts on the subject as they seemed to be daring the other to look away first as they didn't back down, "And maybe there wouldn't be a panic at all, except from the Laramer Bloc. I prefer to give people more credit than how they would react in a bad movie plot."

To her merit, she nodded slowly, looking deep in thought as she supplied slowly, "Perhaps."

The discussion was cut short when the elevator dinged and the white noise generator switched off as the doors opened to a crowded corridor. It was shoulder-to-shoulder Elves, and we just added to the mass migrating toward the open Council Chamber doors. The guards were checking IDs and turning away spectators who would normally be allowed in to sit in the back set of risers with the representatives of the non-voting clans. How had they even known an emergency session had been called?

I'm pretty sure I wasn't the only one who was wondering if the narrowed eyes of Mrs. Havashire were an indication. I would hazard a guess that after this meeting, there was likely to be an investigation as to who in the Senior Council was leaking information to the outside.

She just dragged Tana and me past the guards, giving him a cross look when he started to protest, holding his pad up as if to indicate he was checking names against the list. But he shrank back at the glare from one of the two most powerful women on the Council.

Tana prompted in amusement, "You have to teach me how you do that, Auntie." Then as if remembering where we were, she amended, "Mrs. Havashire."

The woman chuckled and said, "It's something your girlfriend here has in spades, Tanaliashia, the force of will." She winked at us and then shooed us forward toward my seat at the far end of the Chamber as she veered off to the set of risers to the right where her husband, Dimitri Havashire already waited.

I turned back to look at the old secretary's desk, where the second oldest Elf on the planet stood, faking his slight hunch. Claude Blackwood looked to be as ancient as he was, over the theoretical maximum of three hundred years an Elf could live. He winked at me.

Did I mention the man is Faker McFakey, from Fakersville? Playing the doddering old Elf was actually a deviously powerful tool he wielded like a master. You wouldn't believe what people say around him when they think he has problems remembering his last sentence to them. And for some unfathomable reason, he's let both Tana and me in on his little subterfuge.

I sat at my seat with its little railed-in area that matched the huge, railed, opposing risers of the other voting clans that lined either side of the Chamber. Tana opted to stand next to my seat instead of sitting behind me on the riser of the non-voting families who had either sold or contracted off their proxies.

It didn't take more than a couple more minutes before the last of the Senior Council made their way in to be seated, and the corridor was still crowded with spectators and the assistants and families of the Council Members. Some shouting things like, "I thought the vote on the asinine motion the Riicathi girl made wasn't until next week," or "Why the secrecy?" and "I can't believe our Valentine's dinner was ruined by that Riicathi."

Again, why did everyone just assume I was the reason we were all here? Well, in a way I was, but that's beside the point. Cthulhu knows I'm going to start getting a complex here.

Claude stood and we could hear his bones creaking over the gathered crowd as he shuffled slowly to the door controls and the doors swung smoothly closed with a resounding boom as they sealed in the frame. Then he tapped a control and the blue light above the door illuminated as the military-grade white sound curtain draped around the Chamber.

He appeared to get confused until he looked back, eyes widening in surprise at the gathered Council, then he shuffled back to his desk, and everyone leaned forward as he started to lower himself, tendons and bones creaking until everyone started breathing again as he successfully sat, looking proud of himself, the faker.

People were already raising their voices, demanding to know why an emergency session was called. Evander Laun looked around and then exchanged a look with the Havashires across the aisle, they inclined their heads and Evander struck his gavel three times. "We will have order in the Chamber. Any further outbursts will see you escorted from these proceedings."

Now that, was a threat those gathered listened to since the bulk of them just had to be at the center of everything. Everyone settled and quieted as they all to a one were looking around to see if everyone else was as uninformed as they were about things.

Marcillia spoke when there was relative silence in the room, "I'm sure all of you have received the bulletin about the extradition request from the Ethiopian military for the woman accused of aiding Elves to escape their country?" There were nods and murmurs of assent. "We were shocked to hear that there were still Aelftus in the Elf-hostile country. Giving rise to questions about whether there were still some of our people still in hiding in the other Laramer Bloc countries."

Natalia Havashire was taking in which Council Members picked up the thread in that odd power-sharing the two families did in the Chamber. "As this woman was helping our people, we've had our legal staff working tirelessly to figure out what kind of aid we could give her while not violating the Reveal Accords. As we know her extradition would most likely lead to her execution... for helping Elves to escape and survive. So we needed a solution to grant her sanctuary."

Evander looked around and said, "But many revelations have come to light in the past few hours. The woman labeled an 'Elf

Sympathizer' by the Bloc, Diedre James, has been located by Senior Council Member Killisha Renner-Riicathi. And it turns out, the woman all thought to be Sapien is in fact Aelftus..."

He paused as people gasped. I was taking in which Council Members had seemed almost disinterested in what was being said until it was revealed Diedre is Elf, and which members seemed to be concerned the whole time. For the most part, there weren't many surprises as I've pretty much already had most of them categorized that way from the way they reacted to my championing the Dearmadta and my latest motion to give the voting shares back to their original owners.

Then Natalia dropped the bomb. "Not only is she Aelftus but Diedre James in fact, actually Diedre Riicathi." And the Chamber exploded into chaos, dozens of voices shouting out questions over each other.

She simply patted the air in front of her, and everyone quieted down, listening intently now. "In fact, she has hidden away in a safe house with her children." She beamed a smile at everyone. "The Riicathi can add four more to their rolls!" There were actually some cheers and applause at that for the resurrected line all thought once had died out.

This got Dimitri to lightly tap his gavel, quieting everyone as he explained, "So this news makes everything much more straightforward, with Diedre Riicathi being one of our own, and thus eligible for protections under the Reveal Accords. This emergency session has been called because we must act fast before the Ethiopians or even elements of the US government can locate her before we formalize this."

He looked around. "So now we must vote on that formality. I put it to the members of the International Elf Council, do we extend asylum to the Elf who risked all to save more of our own? Yea or Nay?"

Marcillia called out, "Those in favor?" A chorus of, "Yea," sounded out. "Those opposed?" All eyes went to one of the most ardent dissenters on the Havashire's side, who I still haven't learned their name yet, but they remained silent.

Tana's aunt tapped her gavel, "It's done. Let the record reflect the unanimous vote in favor of extending asylum to Diedre Riicathi."

We all turned to the main doors, where Claude sat at his secretary's desk, then he dipped a quill in an ink well and we all listened to the scratching and scribbling on a paper as he formalized the vote. Then after he blotted the ink, he picked up a LaunPad and entered it electronically. I have to hand it to the old man, he's fully embraced the modern world, even while still adhering to tradition.

Then Evander spoke in possibly the most serious tone I've heard him use, "That was all we needed for legal to get the wheels rolling everyone, just be prepared for another emergency session once this is resolved since we now know there are Elves still trapped in the Bloc when those hostile countries swore all Elves had been ejected from their borders. Elves look out for Elves, and we need our people... all our people home."

Shouts of agreement rose as he slammed his gavel. "Dismissed. Keep an eye on your messages."

And with that, everyone was standing and started filing out into the crowded corridor beyond when Claude opened the Chamber doors. A couple of Senior Council Members and some of the non-voting family representatives stepped to me and shook my hand or patted my back, congratulating me for the discovery of more people in the Riicathi clan.

I heard Evander on his cell over the commotion, "Mr. Ingels? We have a go. Keep us apprised. I need to organize an extraction for the new Riicathis. We need to get them to Aelftus Sovereign Soil here in the Tower. Can you inform the NYPD liaison that our security will be moving our protectee? Good man." And he disconnected and looked down from the top of the riser to me, and inclined his head. I beamed a smile to the man and inclined my head right back.

This was awesome news that I couldn't wait to share with Diedre and her kids.

And the extraction was supposed to be simple, and go without a hitch... but here we are, running through the streets and alleys of Manhattan, trying to get to Laun Tower in one piece.

Chapter 9 – Preparation

A s I said, it was supposed to be easy as pie. And here I thought the only difficult thing was when the Launs and Havashires caught up with Tana and me before we boarded the elevator. Evander prompted as he nudged his chin to one of the Council waiting rooms just beyond the elevator bank, "Miss Renner. Natalia implied there was more to this than the blush on the surface. Can we have a quick word in private, I know you wish to get back to inform your family about the vote."

"Umm... ok." I shot Natalia a questioning look. I assumed I knew what they wished to talk about... hadn't she already told them? Get with it Kia, you had just shared the other thing about your new family in the elevator before the Council session, when would she have been able to discreetly do that? Unless of course they could communicate telepathically like the Betazoids on Star Trek, and unfortunately, I know there's no such thing as Elf magic.

She rolled her eyes. I swear she knew what was going through my head, the woman has proved to be scarily insightful about a great many things since I met her after I Elfed.

As soon as we were in Tana made a defiant point of not sitting down at the small conference room-style table, instead turning to the four Elves while grasping my hands. Which wasn't out of line as I usually got a lecture from one or more of the four of them whenever they wished to speak in private. Evander sighed at her display and just activated the white noise curtain as the four faced us.

Natalia spoke first, a slight grin playing at the corners of her lips, "Our dear Miss Renner here shared a shocking revelation about the disposition of Diedre Riicathi's son that if discovered may set off a shitload of events which we need to plan for."

Dimitri cocked a brow in interest as he looked from his wife to me. "And how does this shitload of events differ from your regular shitload of unintended events, young Killishia?" Mr. Funnyman was... well ok, he was funny and he knew it.

But his smile was replaced moments later into an expression I couldn't quite read when I just said plainly, "Jacob is a Halfling like me."

Dimitri blinked twice. "Well fuck."

Evander's tone mirrored his, "Just so."

But Marcillia's expression bloomed into a thoroughly amused smile as she chuckled and prompted, "The Riicathi don't do things in half measures, now do you Kia?"

It was Tana who voiced the truth they all knew, no matter how much they wished to postpone it, "It's going to come out now, it's only a matter of time before people start asking the hard questions, especially since even when he manifests his Elvish traits, he looks more or less Sapien still."

Natalia told the others, "Exactly, and we need contingency plans... we were able to bullshit the public where Killishia was concerned, but mostly because she presents as Elf, even with those adorable ears. But if this Jacob looks more Sapien than her..." She trailed off as the other three nodded.

Then she said as she made an ushering motion with one hand as she reached out to the door controls with the other. "Let the girls get back to Kia's family, and we should retire to the Penthouses to speak more in-depth about all the possible ramifications." She hit the controls and the white noise generator silenced and she opened the door. They all filed out as she called back to us, "Keep us in the loop, girls, but not on unsecured channels."

Tana said, "Will do." As I said while I blinked at the whiplash quick meeting that didn't involve a lecture for me. "Um, bye?"

Then I was being dragged along, Tana not speaking until we were in the elevator next to the Launs and Havashires, rocketing up to the penthouse. She engaged the sound curtain and I said before she could say whatever it was she was thinking, "You have to show me how to do that." I indicated the blue glow from the elevator lighting.

She chuckled and said, "It's all in your Council Member briefing packet you still haven't read, Killy." Then she shared, "I know you want to get back to your Grandparents, but it will be a couple of hours at least until Legal gets this all ironed out, and the quickest a proper extraction team can be set up to safely move Diedre's family here will be tomorrow, especially since they will have to coordinate with local law enforcement. Sonia has been asking after you and I thought we could pop in a moment for you to say hi."

I really was eager to get back, but as she said, bureaucratic wheels spin slowly, and I knew she was right. I was simply excited to share the good news with Diedre... she'll be so relieved. So I caved to logic, was she a Vulcan? "I'd love to see her. I wonder if she has another chapter ready for me to sneak into the editors' inboxes at work. I have to tell you, Tanny, I'm hooked. Sonia has a real talent for writing urban fantasy."

She was beaming with pride. "I know, right?" I seriously do not doubt that when she releases her book, Coven Tales, it is going to soar up the bestseller list. And I loved how the protagonist is loosely based on Tana. Her little sister idolizes her.

She was already in her bed in her pajamas when we went up to her room which was attached to the upper family room slash entertainment room, and Tana's room. She hopped up when Tana knocked and then pulled me through the door. The young Laun's lopsided smile on the slack features which were indicative of Kerricyn Syndrome, made my smile make itself known.

"Kia!" She hugged me, which everyone in her family sees as an accomplishment since she hated anyone but her mother or Tana touching her. Then she released me. "It's Valentine's Day. Tana said she couldn't make it tonight to talk about my day because she was having a Valentine's date with you."

She pointed at her bedside table. "Tana got me a card and chocolates in a heart box." Then she contemplated and said in her muted tones, "I'm not supposed to have sweets before I go to bed." Then she held a finger to her lips as she looked at her door, and whispered, "I ate one after I brushed my teeth, it had caramel in it."

I winked and held a finger to my lips, which assured her that her secret would die with me. Well, we just couldn't have that. I sat on the edge of her bed and held open her covers. She slipped in as I told her, "We would love to hear about your day." Tana tucked her in like a burrito and sat next to me on the edge of the bed, and we listened to how her day went until she was yawning and trying to keep her eyes open twenty minutes later.

We slipped out once she was asleep and I glanced at Tana who looked contemplative. I prompted as she dragged me along by our clasped hands, "What is it?"

She wondered aloud, "Since, inevitably, the world is about to find out about Halflings, maybe it's time for the Aelftus to stop hiding other things."

I looked back at her sister's room. Sonia didn't get out of Laun Tower very often, and when she did it was to other properties owned by her family or other Elves. She's never been out in public and has never personally seen some of the things she writes about in her book. Like Central Park. All because the Elves have presented to the world the pretty, perfect facade that Elves are superior, which includes the fallacy that Elves don't get sick, nor are they susceptible to Sapien afflictions. So in effect, Sonia is a modern sheltered child.

It would be a wonderful thing if Sonia could go out to see all the wonders of the city, instead of just reading about them, or looking at pictures or videos of them. "I swear to Xena Warrior Princess that I'll be the first to show her around her city if the Aelftus stopped selling the 'perfect' facade."

"You're such a geek, Killy."

"Hey, you got the reference, so the geek blade cuts both ways, woman."

She snickered as we reached the elevators again, "God you're cute, Kia."

I felt my cheeks burning as I tucked a strand of hair behind my ear. Then blurted, "Doh!" at her look of amusement at the habit I'm trying to break.

Just as we stepped into the elevator, and selected the lobby, my cell started to buzz. I looked down at it then squinted an eye in mock pain as I answered, my eyes on my girl, "Detective De Luca, to what do I..."

"Stow it, Renner. A little heads-up would have been nice. I had to hear about it from the rant my C.O. just went on."

I asked, "Umm... sorry, Sofia?"

"You're damn right, sorry, Sofia."

I glanced at Tanny who had a brow cocked, the silver of her multiple piercings on that brow shining in the light in the ceiling of the elevator car. I mouthed 'sorry' to her. I know she gets jealous whenever I speak with De Luca.

Then I prompted, knowing the most likely answer, but I just wanted to be sure, "And just what am I apologizing for this time?"

She made an exasperated sound as my stomach was left behind by the rapid descent of the express elevator. "That somehow you have the wanted fugitive from Ethiopia, and now we're tasked with a protection detail because she's not Sapien like we all thought. God damn Reveal Accords."

"Hey now, that's not fair. You already shared with me how distasteful you found it that the NYPD was obligated to assist a hostile nation to extradite someone who was only trying to help people escape their borders."

Sofia huffed out a breath and I could imagine her closing her eyes and pinching the bridge of her nose. "I know, you're right. I'm just a little riled up from my boss accusing me of not giving him a heads up on this clusterfuck." She added, "I'm actually relieved that the Elf Council can shield the woman with sanctuary and asylum under the Accords. It is going to rankle the Bloc that our hands are tied now, and that's the only bright spot here."

"That and a woman whose only crime is trying to get people to safety, and she won't be summarily executed now by the Ethiopian government?"

"Yeah that. You're a pain in my ass, Killishia, you know that?"

I glanced at a now amused-looking Laun, and nodded to the air as I shared, "I've been told I have that effect on people."

She said in a much calmer tone, "We're coordinating with your people now, and it's sounding as if we're going to roll around noon since we have to pull in some resources, and Homeland is crawling up our asses about the whole thing. I guess your lawyer types are stonewalling them and waving around subsections of the Accords in their faces."

I snorted. "Yeah, that would be Aldrich and his team."

"Next time, Renner, don't hang me out to dry." And she ended the call. I looked at my cell as the doors opened and I shrugged at my girl.

She prompted, "Next time?"

"Oh shush, you've nothing to be jealous about."

Ivan was still there, waiting for me to re-emerge. "Hi, big guy." I stuck my thumb out like I was hitchhiking, "My grandparents?

He nodded. "Da." Then he made an ushering motion to us as he inclined his head to my girl, "Aryon. The Minya requests you re-enable the proper tracking on your phone if you are to accompany Miss Kia tonight."

She grinned like a loon, clicking her tongue piercing on her teeth. "So they're calling you now, to get messages to me, huh?"

He just rolled his eyes and we loaded into the waiting SUV and were off to Grams and Gramp's place to share everything that happened with Diedre and her children. I panicked for a moment since my present for Tana was in the SUV, only... it wasn't. The back was empty when we got in. Had it even been there earlier tonight? I swear the Cookie Twins were magicians in another life.

Chapter 10 – Special Report

The news was met with what looked like profound relief as Deidre's shoulders sagged and she exhaled long and hard. She reached out a hand to squeeze my shoulder. "Thank you Killiashia. You've come through beyond my greatest hope. I can breathe easy now knowing my children will be safe."

Tana offered, "All the details are being hammered out by the powers that be, and it sounds like the extraction will be just after noon tomorrow. My parents are making the diplomatic suite of rooms available for you and your children just below the penthouse levels. They're yours to use until official asylum papers can be filed with the international courts in the next few days."

Then she looked around, moving a hand palm up encompassing her children and assuring them, "Nobody can touch you while you're on Aefltus sovereign territory in Laun Tower and Havashire Spire."

Jacob said to his sisters with all the enthusiasm that is standard issue for all teens, "See? I told you Killishia could do it. She's the head of the Riicathi and a Council Member, they listen to her. See? We have potential too even though we're just Halflings."

I winced at the 'just' part. Charity smirked and teased as only a sibling can, "We never said she couldn't, just that you couldn't, pipsqueak."

"Hey! I'm taller than you girls now and..."

Deidre pinched the bridge of her nose, "Jacob, please stop. And girls, you're adults now, try acting like it?"

Then she informed me, "My children will stay at the Tower, I need to organize a team to get back into Ethiopia to get the last of the Elves out and free the ones they took prisoner when they raided the safe house... I will not see them executed in my stead."

Grandpa Riicathi shook his head and told her, "One thing at a time, first your family needs to get to the safety of the tower while asylum is formally in place. Then, this needs to be brought to the Council..."

He indicated me with a nudge of his chin. "Now that the Council is working with us instead of hunting us as we had assumed, maybe it's time to seek help in the matter. Elves help Elves, and while their teams are mediocre at best in their combat skills, they are quite efficient. And they have something we lack, diplomatic resources. So again, one step at a time."

She just stared at him then broke eye contact first and chuckled. "Emit, you sound just like my father."

Mercy chimed in, "He does sound like grandpa, doesn't he?"

Grandma Riicathi offered, "But he does make a good point." She absently rested a hand on her belly.

She lifted her hands above her shoulders and waved them off. "We'll see. The Council..." She looked at Tana. "No offense... has proven less than reliable, allowing this to happen to begin with instead of insisting upon allowing time for the Elves to get out of the country the rebel government overthrew or allowing teams in to facilitate the extraction of the families trapped in a now hostile country."

My girl shrugged it off and said plainly, "They didn't have Killy here stirring the pot back then. Plus, you'd be amazed at what my parents and the Havashires are capable of when it comes to the welfare of the Aelftus."

It wasn't long after that Tana and the boys were dropping me off at my place. We lingered on the front porch we shared with my neighbors, and she leaned in and whispered, her breath hot on my face and lips a bare millimeter from mine, "Happy Valentine's Day, Killishia."

I winced and promised, "I'm sorry about today. I'll make it up to you tomorrow night?"

She chuckled and our lips met, causing me to sigh into the gentle kiss. She left me there on the porch, inappropriately aroused, lips parted as another sigh escaped me... "Oh, ok."

I wasn't surprised to find my gift to Tana sitting in the middle of my room when I made it upstairs after Barney greeted me with his wagging tail excitement.

My dreams were conflicted, one leaving me feeling frantic, with Elves cowering in fear in some faraway land, followed by one of my favorites which involved Tanny and myself.

The house was silent, and when my ears swiveled to pick up any sound inside, all I could hear was Barney's breathing where he slept with his shaggy bulk across my feet, and mom's familiar, almost but not quite snore, down the hall. Had I slept through dad waking up and leaving with Gertie? I must have been exhausted.

I did smell coffee being brewed and the telltale aroma of dad's cooking. He had left breakfast for mom and me. I really must have been dead to the world all right. Usually, the smell of coffee would have had my eyes snapping open and me shuffling downstairs for the liquid ambrosia.

Yawning I poured some coffee and looked in the oven in warming mode, where dad left two breakfasts in small covered ceramic ramekins. I had to smile at the little aluminum foil packet that contained a couple of slices of bacon for Barney, who was lazily trotting down, likely following his nose, the sound of the nails on his paws clicking lightly on the stairs preceded him wandering into the kitchen, tail wagging lazily, yawning then shaking himself, his long fur flaring out from the motion.

I rolled my eyes. "You came down for this but not me?" Just like a boy. I scrubbed his ears and deposited the bounty from the foil pouch into his dish. I know, I shouldn't feed the big guy human food, but... he's so cute. He nudged me aside and proceeded to wolf down the offering as I chuckled at him.

Then I moved into the living room with my food and flopped down onto the sinfully comfy, overstuffed couch mom found at a thrift store down the street. I flipped on the television with the sound virtually muted to not wake mom, and I watched the early morning WTRL news while I dug into the Mediterranean omelet dad had made, savoring the chopped tomatoes and onions in it.

I fed Barney a nibble of the egg since he can't have onions, when he joined me on the couch, laying across my legs and effectively pinning me down with his bulk. I swear, ever since we rescued him and brought him into our home, he's thought he was a lap dog.

Balancing the ramekin on his back, I took a sip from the hot coffee, letting the taste flow over my tongue before swallowing. Coffee has become so much more of an experience since I Elfed and was one of the few times I enjoyed my slightly enhanced senses. Then I was blinking and setting the coffee mug on the side table when a news report came in.

"What the fluff?"

I was leaning forward on Barney, moving the ramekin to the table too as I watch our early morning anchors give the report, the headline blazing on the screen where video footage was being displayed. That headline? 'Ethiopian Military Authority Demands Turnover of Wanted Terrorist'.

Kamiko Lee was reporting. "At an emergency session of the United Nations, General Yafet Yohannes, the leader of the Ethiopian Military Authority Defense Force, and leaders of the Laramer Bloc have issued demands after receiving actionable intelligence that the International Elf Council is sheltering a wanted fugitive, Deidre James, here in Manhattan."

"James is wanted for terrorist activities including lending aid to illegal Aelftus residents within the borders of Ethiopia's Phyletic Exclusion Zone, backed by the Laramer Bloc leaders. They claim the IEC is in direct violation of international laws in harboring this fugitive, and demand that world leaders respond."

"We'll keep our viewers updated as we learn more about these accusations and who this Deidre James is. This is Kamiko Lee with WTRL News, and we'll be back with today's weather forecast after these commercial messages."

I whispered, "Fuck." No other word would do.

Then winced when mom said from upstairs, "Language young lady." I didn't even have it in me to whine that I was a grown woman. How had the disposition of Deidre leaked to the Ethiopians before the Council officially declared her and her family protected under the Accords... which legal was going to do the moment they set foot in Laun Tower?

And the calls started coming in. "Hi, Tobias. No, I can't talk about that now. Yes, and I still can't talk about... hang on, please. I have another incoming call from the Council now." I switched over to the incoming call as the station manager started to protest, "Ummm... Hello Mr. Laun."

"Killishia, Deidre Riicathi's disposition has been leaked. The extraction team is coordinating with NYPD as we speak to get her family to safety now."

He paused for three heartbeats and my eyes widened before I blurted, "You don't think I leaked it to those Bloc assholes, do you? I have a few choice words for you if you do, sir."

He exhaled in exasperation. "We don't know how the information was leaked, since we've been keeping a tight lid on it, and legal was waiting until they got the all clear before submitting the paperwork to the new military coup leaders of Ethiopia."

When he paused again, I wondered if I misread his first pause, then he asked, "Is Tanaliashia with you? We've not been able to locate her since the story broke."

I heard a vehicle stop at the curb, a car door, and familiar footsteps approaching the door at a run. "Gotta go, sir. She just arrived."

"Killis..." I disconnected and just said, "Come in." Tana burst through the door. "We have to move now, Killy."

Mom called out, "You girls go ahead, I'll meet you at Roberto and Irene's." I would have worried about her if I didn't know that behind her erratic and sometimes bizarre behavior, she was a highly skilled Mahta-quárë practitioner even though she preferred, umm... other methods of self-defense. She was particularly fond of the taser and air horn in her shoulder bag. I did mention just how awesome my mom was, right?

I was already dashing toward the stairs when my cell buzzed again, "I'll be right down." I looked at my screen. Crap on a Dalek, it was Detective De Luca. I looked at the accept slider before ultimately sending it to voicemail, I could call her back in the car.

The next one I answered though as I quickly discarded my sleepwear onto my messy floor, tangling my feet up in my pants and falling face first into the bed while I started dressing in a rush. I mumbled into the bed, "Hi Lis. Not a good time."

"Ah, so you're aware. Just making sure you weren't about to be blindsided." Then before I could say anything, she said, "I'll meet you at Laun Tower."

Before I could tell her she didn't need to do that, she preemptively countered, "What are work wives for? I'll provide the moral support, you provide the chaos."

"Love ya."

"Right back at ya, Elfette. Rodriguez out." And she hung up. I have such an awesome bestie.

Then I was flying downstairs and cocked a brow at Tana who was sharing the last of my breakfast with Barney. She didn't look repentant in the least as she grabbed my hand and dragged me to the door. Ivan was waving me toward the SUV in front of Tana's car of the week. From her family's private fleet.

If I didn't already know time was of the essence, the way his lips were pressed together in a thin line and the urgency painted on his face would have done the trick. "Hurry, Miss Kia, Aryon, the extraction team rolls in less than thirty minutes."

We wordlessly slipped into the back seat and the vehicle was in motion with Pietor at the wheel before Ivan fully closed the door and we had our seatbelts on, for the short ride to the Renner safe house.

I texted both sets of grandparents, and they were already aware of what was going on. Ivan had already got three teams of Elvish Special Ops there while Diedre and her children were prepping for the move. They were just waiting for the NYPD escort detachment to arrive before moving out.

The urgency of the situation settled in when I overheard a
report to Ivan, that US Homeland Security, the FBI, and the
military were heading into the city before the 'goddamn elves
cause an international incident by harboring a fugitive from a
hostile nation'. The only saving grace was that nobody knew
where we had Deidre at the moment, even though our plans to
move her were somehow leaked. Truth be told, that leak was
what truly had me worried since the police weren't going to be
informed of her and her children's location until just before the
extraction.

There was already a lot of activity at Grams and Gramp's
place as we pulled up, and the police were on the way, which
means the possibility of a leak in the location was a distinct
possibility too. But the Bloc couldn't possibly have mobilized
their extraction team with such short notice, could they? And
they wouldn't risk an international incident either, right? I
mean... I prompted Ivan as he unbuckled and stepped out before
us to scan the area before letting us out, "Everyone has to abide
by the Accords, right?"

The big guy gave me a pointed look. Yeah, right, got it. I'm
counting on the same US government that had black ops running
to develop a neurotoxin that only targeted Elves. It had almost
killed me, and the only thing that saved me from that painful

death was the fact I was a Halfling, my Sapien DNA allowing me to fight it off.

And that definitely was against the Reveal Accords. Congress was covering their asses by defunding and disbanding then 'investigating' the supposedly rogue group responsible. So maybe Ivan is right not to put any faith in them honoring the Accords unless the International Elf Council calls them out on it.

So basically the race was on. The moment Diedre's family set foot on any Aelftus property, the asylum stipulations, and Aelftus citizen protections afforded all Elves would be in effect. And the US Government couldn't set foot on Aelftus property, as it was all the sovereign territory we Elves had, being a landless nation. It is the first time I have ever been all for politics since they usually just eff everything up.

We were rushed into the house, Ivan and Pietor following me this time. They always made a point of not coming inside the Renner houses, giving us a semblance of privacy, and since they knew about the nature of this house, I suppose it was plausible deniability for the Cookie Twins. But this wasn't a time for subtlety.

My ears swiveled toward Ivan's brother and I heard over Pietor's earbud that the police detachment, led by Detective De Luca was five minutes out. And the hidden door under the stairs opened and everyone started coming out, Gramps Renner paused when he saw the Russians standing there, seeing them all emerging from the hidden staircase, then he exhaled and ushered the rest out into the ground floor living room as he greeted me, "Kia."

I waved awkwardly from my hip as I squinted in apology, "Gramps... sorry."

He chuckled and then as one, all heads swung toward the door, ears swiveling that way and I held a halting hand out. "It's just mom, that's her Volkswagen."

She started to argue with the guards outside the house, but Ivan just touched his earbud, "Let her through."

Mom was grumbling, "Damn skippy let her through." She eyeballed the big man mountains as she shut the door behind her. There was no give in her expression and it made Ivan smile, knowing just how lethal, the deceptively 'mom' looking woman was.

She poked him in the ribs to punctuate, then winged a thumb toward the door, "Your overzealous platypuses out there need some manners."

"Da, I will take it under advisement, Mrs. Renner."

His amusement... didn't amuse mom. And she just held her arms out wiggling her fingers toward Tana and me. We obliged and she hugged us both to her before releasing us and turning to the now-assembled group. She winged a thumb again, "Saw the police three blocks up, running silent. They'll be here in a moment. It would be a hell of a thing if they could get to crime scenes this fast instead of detouring to the donut shop."

"Mom, be nice."

"I'm the nicest person I know, Kia dear. Well second nicest, your father is packing up the truck and said he'll meet us all at Laun Tower."

Then she shook her head. "The news reports are causing a stir, right before I left to follow you here, they mentioned how people are crowding the streets around Laun Tower and Havashire Spire, trying to get a look at the so-called fugitive and terrorist they are reported to be protecting."

What?

She added, "Last I heard was there seem to be two groups clashing over it, the pro-Elf people and a smaller crowd of those calling for justice and to hand over Deidre."

Son of a radioactive spider, the skewed news reports are fanning the flames and this is suddenly turning into something that could spiral out of control.

I held a finger up as I pulled out my cell and called the station manager's direct line, he answered on the first ring, "Kia, I was wondering when you'd be calling. Does the Council have any..."

"Mr. Klien, we have to stop running the story. It isn't factual, you're only getting the manufactured facts a rogue nation is feeding the public. WTRL is even reporting on the chaos it is stirring up at Laun Tower."

He sounded consolatory as he said, and I could imagine him shaking his head slowly, "We can only report the information as we uncover it, and so far the Elf Council is stonewalling and refusing to comment."

"Stop fishing man, you're about as subtle as a porcupine in a balloon factory wearing pants."

"Why would it be wearing... never mind. I'm a reporter, rooting out the story is what we do. You're a reporter too." Then he added, "Probationary."

I exhaled in resignation, my shoulders slumping. "Sir. I can supply the real story about the so-called fugitive in a couple of hours. Right now we need to tamp down the fire the reports are causing. I know the other stations won't but WTRL has the most viewers."

Before he could interrupt, I added, "Off the record?"

He hesitated and muttered, "Damn it, Renner." Then he repeated, "Off the record."

All eyes around me were wide in disbelief and I shrugged to them all and then told the man, "This Deidre James, is not a Sapien as the Laramer Bloc believes, she is an Elf who is receiving asylum with the Aleftus nation as per the Reveal Accords. And we need to assure her safety before I can provide you an exclusive as to the false accusations and charges against her, as well as the plight of multiple Elf families."

I finished with, "Just give us two hours, you can even report it is a developing story and that new facts have come to light that cast doubt on the story the Ethiopian Military Authority Defense Force is supplying the public. We need to diffuse the demonstrations in front of the Aelftus towers now."

He repeated, "She's an Elf?" The man was too good at his job and could read into situations with frightening insight, he almost whispered, "Dear lord, she's not on Aelftus territory yet." Then he muttered, "Shit." Then this time he did whisper, "And the feds that are converging are wanting to hand her over before there's an international incident."

"Yes."

"What a cluster-fuck. Well, it is you, after all, so of course it's going to be convoluted."

"Hey, sir."

I heard him exhale then he almost growled out, "I don't know why I stick my neck out for you, Renner, but I'll craft a report to try to alleviate the flames around the powder keg." Then he said pointedly, "Two hours." And he disconnected.

I said to the air, "Umm... bye?" Then I looked around to many cocked brows. "Hey now, we needed to get the reports stopped. If violence breaks out before we even get there..." I left it hanging.

As a group, they seemed to all reluctantly agree with me. And I addressed the elephant in the room, "He's good people and will honor his word. He won't leak."

Tana countered, "He's a reporter."

"So am I."

"Probationary."

"Come on, you too, woman?" Then I assured her, "He's a reporter who won't steamroll over innocent people to get a story."

And any further conversation was dropped as we heard four vehicles pull up and stop at the curb and multiple car doors. I pointed toward the door, "It's showtime." I looked at Deidre's family, "Everyone ready?"

They nodded and Ivan took over as Pietor greeted De Luca at the door before she could knock.

Chapter 11 – They Were Everywhere

Without much pomp and circumstance, we were on the move. I was surprised how seamlessly Council Security worked with the NYPD... almost as if they trained on drills for this sort of thing.

And our caravan was led by two police cruisers into Manhattan, over the bridge instead of the tunnel, since surface streets allowed better security or something like that. One unmarked police SUV driven by Sofia trailed the five Aelftus vehicles.

We didn't take a direct route, and I knew why once I overheard over Ivan's earbud about back-channel chatter on the mercenary dark web that an open contract had been issued for Deidre James last night by 'interested parties'. The bastards put a price on my cousin's head.

And as anxious as the atmosphere was in the SUV with her and her children, Tana and me, and the Cookie Twins up front. It looked to be much ado about nothing as we traveled smoothly through the city.

I sighed audibly and just smiled at the twins and Jacob in the third-row seating, when the world erupted into a cacophony of sound, as we were thrown in our seats to the side, my shoulder striking the door that crushed in toward me. The sound of armor plating bending and bulletproof glass cracking but not breaking as my head hit it, my seat belt the only thing preventing me from more damage as the SUV was pushed sideways, tires squealing and protesting, off the street and into an alley by the huge garbage truck that hit us going thirty or forty miles per hour when it came streaking out of the opposing alley mouth.

My vision was swimming and my ears were ringing as the tires caught and the SUV flipped sideways, once, then twice, before settling on its hood. Someone was yelling out orders, and something about, "They've isolated our vehicle."

My head cleared enough that I realized in my disorientation that we were all hanging upside down by our seatbelts. Tana was repeating my name as she dropped to the roof of the vehicle at almost the same time Ivan, Pietor, Deidre, and the twins did. "Killy, are you ok? Come on, we have to move."

What? Oh yes. I was floundering for the seatbelt button while Charity and Mercy were helping a stunned Jacob out of his. Tana pressed the button and cushioned me the best she could when I fell to the roof. I wiped the blood from my eyes with a shaky hand as she was asking, "Are you ok, Killy?"

I took a deep breath to clear my head and nodded through the excruciating headache, "Yeah, I think so. What's happening?"

Ivan kicked his door twice before it flew open, metal screeching. He rolled out and automatic gunfire sounded as he rolled to his feet and was already firing his pistol while Pietor was snapping instructions, "Everyone out, stay low, use the vehicle for cover, and stay behind Ivan and me. We'll be moving fast."

He drew his weapon then as if an afterthought, he reached down and pulled another gun from a little holster at his ankle and held it out to Deidre who accepted it smoothly and manipulated it like she had been born to it as she checked the magazine and verified a round was chambered.

The man looked around at all of us as he crawled back to us to kick open the back door. "Ok, on three. One, two, three." And we were running.

I could hear De Luca behind the garbage truck that had stopped diagonally across the alley opening, blocking us in, as her people were pinned down by gunfire on that side too. She was calling for backup, then said, "Fuck it, cover me." And I lost track of her voice as rapid semi-automatic fire rang out.

A moment later I was spinning off to the side, grabbing Tana on my way past to twist her out of the way of incoming gunfire from three men in tactical gear and body armor, who stepped out of shadowed doorways. The world had brightened and seemed to slow as muzzle flash started to bloom, and I had moved on instinct, feeling a barrage of bullets whiz past where we had been standing, one catching the back of my shirt and going through the fabric.

I noted Jacob had pulled his sisters down to avoid the strafing fire too as Pietor and Deidre just walked steadily forward through the maelstrom of automatic weapons fire, their guns firing just twice each. And as my twist ended with us looking the same direction we had before, the three men were falling, red holes in their foreheads.

I didn't have time to be horrified at that and the efficiency with which the two had ended them because five others swarmed around the corner into the alley. And Grams and Gramps Riicathi dropped down behind them, from fire escapes on either side of the alley.

With brutal efficiency, Gramps put one in an arm bar, overextending the man's arm, and popping it out of the socket with a wet thucking sound. The man was screaming in pain and reflexively pulled the trigger on his automatic rifle, striking two of his allies in the chest. Knocking them down, their body armor absorbing most of the impact, but blood was pumping from one of the downed men's chest, when with a popping crunch, Gramps twisted the head of the man he had just released, almost completely around, and dropping him.

At the same time, Grams lunged and ducked under the man's aim as he fired, her leg sweeping out Elf fast and impacting his knee as she drove through the space, bending his leg backward in an unnatural angle. And she stood, the heel of her palm striking up and impacting his nose. I could hear cartilage splinter and the man's eyes rolled up as he went slack. Had she just driven the cartilage up into his brain? She hooked his arm as he started to fall and flipped him violently over, his body slamming into the last man.

As they went down in a tangle of arms and legs, she stomped the head of the third man Gramps took down. Then she calmly stepped to the final man as he untangled from his dead compatriot, grabbing his arm and stepping past him and back, twisting the man's arm almost out of its socket as she stopped as he screamed.

Gramps asked, "Who are you people? You're not Ethiopian. How many of you are there?"

The man cursed out in pain in a sharp Germanic-like language I didn't understand, and to my surprise, Grams snapped out at him in the same language. The man cursed at her and she moved his arm farther back, I could hear tendons and muscles starting to tear as he bellowed in pain. She asked again and he spat at her. She yanked hard and tissue rended as his arm popped out of the socket. Then Gramps kicked him solidly on the chin, breaking his jaw and knocking the man out with the vicious force of it.

Holy mother of violence, Batman. Mahta-quárë was no joke.
It was violence incarnate and my grandparents were masters in
the art.

Then my grandparents turned to all of us, straightening their
shirts, Grams saying, "Hello. Sorry, we're late. Shall we get
moving? We saw multiple vehicles filled with others dressed like
these blocking the streets and setting up a kill box."

I squeaked out, "Hi? Grams, Gramps? How did you get
here?"

Grandma Riicathi smiled fondly. "You don't think we were
watching, sweetie? Now come on everyone, there's no time. We
have to get through before they get their kill box finalized.
They've only got a minute or two before the area is swarming
with police."

Pietor barked out, "Go!"

And Tana was rubbing her neck as she said to me in awe, "I
got whiplash you moved us out of the way so fast Killy, I couldn't
follow your movement."

I shrugged as we jogged up to the elder Ricathiis. "Jacob
pulled his sisters down just as fast. The rest of you were just
moving slowly."

Charity and Mercy picked up rifles from the bodies at our
feet, and they both stopped Jacob when he tried to grab one.
Mercy shook her head no as she and her sister checked the

magazines in the weapons then took spare clips from one of the men's weapons harnesses.

Deidre stepped up to join the patriarch and matron of my branch of the family, and they inclined their heads at each other and proceeded to the mouth of the alley.

And that brings us back to now, as we jogged up to them, and I panted as we slid to a stop to look out of the alley as we waited for the all-clear from Grams and Gramps Riicathi to proceed to the next alley.

My grandparents dashed out of the alley across the street, being fired on from both directions. Pietor and Deidre looked at the rest of us then she locked eyes with me as Ivan rejoined us, and she said in a voice much calmer than I could believe... how could she not be freaking out as much as I was right now? "When we step out, you need to get Jacob and your girl across, we'll lay down suppressing fire."

And before I could protest, Pietor and Deidre stepped out smoothly on one side of the alley, and Ivan and the twins stepped out the other side, and my ears were punished by the gunshots that were threatening to deafen me as they just slowly sidestepped, their weapons slinging controlled bursts of lead as bullets peppered the lamp posts, parked cars, and newspaper boxes around them.

"Now!" someone yelled and Jacob and I grabbed Tana's hands and ran, dragging her along with us. Was she dragging her feet or... no, my usually graceful girlfriend was stumbling as she tried to keep up with us, and Jacob and I just lifted her off her feet and got to the safety of the other alleyway. I could taste all the adrenaline pumping through my body.

We looked back as the others moved to join us. Ivan stumbled back as a round hit him in the chest, and he got to safety with us. The big man growled and placed a hand over the hole in his dress shirt, then tore it open and the shock and terror I had that he was hit was alleviated when I saw the vest with a round flattened against it.

There was no sign or smell or taste of his blood in the air, and I sighed in profound relief. I've grown to see the Cookie Twins as my overprotective big brothers and it would shatter my heart if one of them got killed protecting me.

Diedre chuckled and said, "That's going to bruise like hell. Ribs?"

He shook his head as he hid a wince, "Nyet, just smarts."

"Well you are a huge target, I'm amazed you avoided getting hit more."

They exchanged feral grins then we were on the move again.

Pietor told us, "These appear to be the mercenaries coming to collect the bounty on you Mrs. Riicathi. How did they know the route we'd take? Or that you weren't already at the tower?"

Those were the questions that we didn't have time to contemplate as more mercenaries and other men in military uniforms I didn't recognize swarmed either end of the alley. They had boxed us in, they were everywhere!

The soldiers must be from the Bloc. They must have flown directly here overnight. Wasn't that like an act of war or something? Foreign military personnel conducting operations on another country's soil?

Just as guns were swinging our way, Pietor threw his entire two hundred and fifty pounds plus frame at a warehouse door, splintering the jamb as the steel door flew inwards. "In, now!" And he started firing back as the first bullets started peppering the asphalt ground and brick walls.

We ducked inside and the Cookie Twins tipped over a huge metal cabinet next to the door to block it as we all scanned the warehouse as we moved away from the door where people started pounding, shooting, and yelling at us.

Now what?

Chapter 12 - Did Someone Order Lunch?

G rams and Gramps dashed off in opposite directions as the five armed ones of our group circled around Jacob, Tanny, and me.

Both my and Tana's cells were buzzing incessantly. Ivan just put out a hand and we handed them to him. He stomped them. Aw man, I really liked that one. I've only owned it for three years now. But I understood, all our electronics except theirs could be tracked.

So we all just stood there, panting as the elder Riicathi in our midst did a quick reconnoiter of the building, looking for a way out that wouldn't involve our bodies becoming ventilated by lead. What I wouldn't give for a communicator and a transporter right about now. Scotty, beam us up.

My muscles started shaking as the adrenaline left my system while we all took a moment to catch our breath until my grandparents returned. Jacob was sitting on a dusty and dilapidated crate and I could see his hands shaking as he clasped them to hide it.

Tana was checking me over, her eyes widening when she found the hole in the back of my shirt. I prompted her, "Are you ok?"

She chuckled. "Am I ok? The question is, are you ok?" Then she sighed and pointed a finger between Jacob and me. "Yes, I'm fine. I still can't get over how fast you are at times... and Jacob is almost as fast as you too. Much faster than any Elf I've ever seen. You two are wonders."

Jacob was looking a little embarrassed over the praise as his sisters were checking him over for injuries. Then when they were satisfied, Charity mussed his hair as Mercy checked their weapons. "Two rounds left and one reload, yours is empty, how many mags do you..."

Charity pulled a magazine from her waistband and showed her it was mangled. "I took a hit. So it's hand to hand for me." She laid the rifle on a crate and then asked, "Mom?"

The matron of their family cleared her gun, ejecting a round and dropping the magazine like she had done it a thousand times. She reinserted the magazine and chambered the round. "One." She handed it back to Pietor. "I saw you two unload all you had. Nice shooting by the way."

Pietor inclined his head and accepted the gun. "Da, you as well. You've trained?"

"Dad insisted I..." she corrected as she nodded at her daughters, "That we do weekly drills at the range because..."

Jacob interjected, sounding as if he were reciting a lesson, "If an enemy is beyond your reach, all the Mahta-quárë in the world is worth shit-all."

Deidre exhaled like all parents did when addressing a misbehaving child, "Language, Jacob."

"Yes ma'am." Then to Tana and me, he added, "They won't let me touch a gun."

His mother said patiently as she reached a hand out to cup his cheek. "Your coordination leaves something to desire, sweetheart. Through no fault of your own. You still need to work on your hand-to-hand drills to increase your reflexes before you handle weapons that can inadvertently kill you or someone else if you fumble with them."

He huffed and nodded reluctantly. "I bet Killishia is allowed to. She's like me, and isn't clumsy like me."

Tana squeaked, covering her mouth to hide her smile, and I noted four or five new rings on her fingers gleaming in the light of the sunlight streaking through high windows near the roof line and the dirt-covered skylights over the mezzanine above. "Killy is the clumsiest woman I know, but her recoveries are grace incarnate. It's your nervous systems being faster than you can process unless adrenaline hits your systems."

I gave her a pouty lip and then smiled at her waggling brows. Then I jumped when my grandparents rejoined us, moving virtually soundlessly even to my Elf ears. Gramps shared, "There are five exits, we blocked them all before their teams got to them, they won't hold long."

Grams supplied, "The roof has clear views of the streets around us. They've blocked off everything and are clashing with the NYPD group. Reinforcements are two minutes out by the sound of it, so they are going to rush us now as soon as they make it through one of the barricaded doors."

Ivan asked, "Are there nearby rooftops?"

Gramps nodded slowly, looking between me and Jacob. "There's a four-story walk-up on the other side of the alley that we could probably jump to... most of us that is."

Damn... being a Halfling is endangering the entire group. They could get away, but... I looked at Jacob and sighed in understanding. Deidre was going nowhere without her son. And the woman asked, "Any response to the call we sent out last night, Audrey?"

What call?

Grams shook her head as she pulled out a cell and held it up, wiggling it back and forth for emphasis. I was about to protest that she had a cell that could be traced but the Cookie Twins didn't confiscate it. Then I realized that the Bloc wouldn't know they were involved let alone tracking their cells. And she asked, "Would they come and expose themselves?"

"They will come."

Who will come? And I was about to ask when we heard two doors being breached and shouts and sounds of multiple sets of feet running our way. Ivan was snapping his fingers and making a motion for us to get behind them as all the fighters moved forward.

Then I heard something, blurting, "There's another way out."

I pointed at a manhole cover twenty feet from us beside a floor drain, where I could hear water flowing below it. The sewers. Pietor was dashing to it and reached fingers between some holes in the cover and then with a strained grunt, pried it up and let it clatter to the floor as he looked in.

Then he was motioning us over as dozens of men came pouring into the open space, and weapons started swinging our way as Ivan was shouting, "Everyone in, now!"

With whupping sounds, dozens of knives spun down from above, knocking guns from hands, and some embedding in necks or hands as around two dozen Elves dropped from the mezzanines above, and I had to blink as an Elf with short, rounded ears, and hazel eyes glanced our way. Another Halfling!

And as we were all jumping into the sewage moving through the tunnel below, I saw violence at an unimaginable scale being unleashed as men screamed in agony before gurgling last breaths, and those who still had their guns in hand started firing indiscriminately at the newcomers who moved Elf fast avoiding the shots.

I jumped and was caught by Pietor as my feet hit the sewage, and my gag reflex had me dry heaving from the overwhelming stench that was just amplified by my Aelftus senses. Then we were all down and running... wait, where were my grandparents? They stayed behind to cover our retreat with those other Elves?

I gasped out, my eyes watering from the foul odor that smelled like the armpit of hell, "Who were those Elves? Council? There was another Halfling."

Diedre, who was pinching her nose closed, eyes watering as we sloshed along, through the water and sludge and things I didn't want to know about bumping into my shins, said, "No, not Council. That was the rest of the Riicathi. We sent out a call last night, just in case, and they answered."

"The... the rest of the Riicathi? I thought your family was the last."

She chuckled and shared, "When did I ever say that, Kia?" Then she winked at me. There were more Riicathi? And another Halfling... was it something about our clan?

After two blocks Ivan went up a rung ladder and pushed up a manhole cover and looked around. "Clear, everyone up, we must hurry. We are three blocks from the Tower."

We could hear gunfire from two directions, and police and ambulance sirens. And the sounds of bullhorns calling for people to shelter in place. It sounded like a war zone or some sort of disaster movie. Were the Laramer Bloc not afraid of the repercussions of launching a manhunt in the United States? Or were they emboldened by their respective rogue military coups in their countries, thinking that is how it was everywhere?

And a nearby police radio talking about evacuating a four-block radius from where our vehicle had been rammed. Part of me was relieved that it was Sofia's voice... she was still ok.

Ivan looked at us all as we darted into yet another alley for some cover. "More Council Special Ops teams are being mobilized from Havashire Spire. The National Guard is arriving at Laun Tower and not allowing entry or exit, barring our teams from there. They're heading down into the subway station to make egress there."

Pietor nodded and said, "We should be able to make it there, it seems most of the resistance is behind us now."

We slipped out of the alley and started down the street, under some scaffolding from a building renovation and plywood walkway covered with layers of playbills, toward the two looming towers and salvation. Just as four SUVs turned the corner behind us and came screaming down the road to skid to a violent halt as they spread out and turned virtually sideways to block the entire road and sidewalk.

We picked up the pace, weaving between the scaffolding and the parked cars, just as sporadic gunfire started peppering the cars and the sidewalk. And we skidded to a halt, half of us sliding between two vehicles while the rest slid behind another as four more SUVs came barreling around the corner, coming to a screeching halt, sending blueish plumes of smoke from the tires to block our path. One of the vehicles swung too wide and crashed into a parked truck.

There was no place left to run, they had us. My heart was pounding in my chest as Tana grasped my hand tightly, looking fiercely protective of me as she pulled me tighter to her side. I let out a shaky breath then... was someone blaring Fleetwood Mac's "Don't Stop" somewhere?

An engine revved and roared as a massive electric yellow Humvee slammed into two of the SUVs before the men could get out. One vehicle was sent skidding and slamming into the SUV which had misjudged the turn, crushing a man halfway out his door. The other spun and flipped, rolling over onto its side, and blocking the men from the last vehicle.

Issac!

Then Lisa's Elf boyfriend slammed the Humvee into reverse and laid waste to that one too. If it weren't for the fact Issac

Walker owned a military-style Humvee instead of one of those cheap civilian knockoffs, his vehicle would have been trashed from the impacts.

He raced down the road to just past us and torqued the wheel over to interpose the Humvee between the shooters behind us and where we were pinned down.

Lisa slipped out of the passenger door and Issac followed. My insane bestie, who was endangering herself there, was screaming out to us all, "What are you doing just sitting there, people? Time to make like brave Sir Robin and run away! Run away!"

You can't argue with sound logic like that, so we all ran away, using the Humvee for cover. And just as we were passing the trashed cars, Ivan and Pietor along with Diedre, making short work of the stunned mercenaries.

Gertie came to a stop in the intersection, tires catching and screeching a little as dad called out the window from the driver's seat, "Did someone order lunch?" He was motioning urgently with his hand, "Come on Itty Bit, get everyone in the back. Let's go people! Go go go!"

And we all loaded up and made our moderately paced getaway, Gertie's engine straining as we all stood, packed like sardines, as cooking implements and ingredients fell from their places in the swaying vehicle as dad took corners faster than would be advisable, the tires on one side momentarily leaving the ground in the first high-speed turn at the first intersection. We only had a block to go in our escape food truck when dad stopped in the middle of the road.

Son of a Kryptonian Pyramid Scheme, could we not catch a break?

Some military vehicles blocked the road ahead, and some men in black suits were pointing at Gertie and men started mobilizing.

Dad was starting to shift into reverse when I reached past the tightly packed bodies to rest a hand on his arm. "Wait, I know where we are. Tana, are Elf-owned businesses also considered Aelftus territory?"

"Yes, by necessity, why do you..."

"Everyone out, trust me."

And oddly, nobody questioned me, the back door of Gertie swung open and we poured out as the military vehicles swarmed toward us. I ran just two doors down and yanked open the glass door with gold lettering on it. Everyone followed and then started barricading the doors with benches and tables.

I looked to Ivan, "Tell Aldrich to pull the trigger now! We're on Aelftus Sovereign Soil, asylum is in effect now. Deidre and her children have sanctuary. And have him call Homeland now to call off the military jackals out there!"

He was already on task as everyone looked around in confusion then realization was apparent in their widened eyes at the colorful menu of the bakery we were in, with the big logo above it proudly proclaiming this high-end establishment as "Jericho's Fine Pastries". Owned by the Jericho clan.

Then I noticed the Elf workers cowering behind the counter and a few customers who were huddled in the corner who were likely stuck here because of the shelter-in-place order. I felt my cheeks heating as I waved awkwardly from a hip, and tucked a strand of hair behind my ear as I lamely said, "Oh. Hi. Don't mind us, Elf Council Business and all... you know how it is."

Chapter 13 - Uncle Sam

We could hear the military forming a perimeter in front of the Bakery, and the order to cover the back, sending multiple vehicles to the alley behind the building.

Charity asked with humor as she and Mercy went behind the counter, politely excusing themselves as they rummaged for weapons, coming up with nothing but some knives, "Is your life always so... exciting, Killishia?"

I shrugged when multiple people snorted. "This is pretty much a normal Tuesday for me now." Then I spun on Lisa. "What in the nine circles of hell are you and Issac doing here? You could have been killed."

She shrugged, looking a little sheepish, "You're welcome."

I sighed, closed my eyes, and centered myself. "Thank you, and thank you, Issac, you may have just saved all our lives."

He chuckled in his Australian accent, "No worries mate, though my insurance on my ride likely won't cover this." He was all grins. Yes, I approved of my bestie's man.

I know I should have been thinking about something else at that moment, but I just had to ask him, "What kind of rescue music is Fleetwood Mac, anyway?"

He was all grins as Lisa rolled her eyes so hard I may have heard it. "Got addicted to the classics since it's all my parents and grands listened to when I was growing up. Plus the added fact that Stevie Nicks is from the Walker clan."

Whaaa? "Stevie Nicks is an Elf?"

I looked over at my bestie and she shrugged and shared, "Hey now, at least he's pretty. I tried telling him something with more bite as We Will Rock You was more appropriate. I mean, boys, what you gonna do? Right?"

It was dad asking, "What's wrong with Fleetwood Mac?" that finally broke the tension and everyone chuckled nervously as we wondered what was next.

Tana started rubbing my arms when an involuntary shiver went through me as I burned off the last adrenaline dump. How much of that stuff could my body produce anyway? Then most of us were wincing when the bullhorns started.

"This is the US Government. The building is surrounded. You are in breach of U.S. and International laws by harboring a fugitive. Surrender her now or we will take her by force. All individuals who have been accomplices in hiding her will be brought up on charges."

I looked over to Ivan expectantly as he was speaking with legal. The man shrugged and whispered, "Homeland security and the international courts have been informed. These men should be getting the call if they haven't already."

Lis and I chimed out in unison, "Unless they already have and are ignoring it."

I took a step forward as I realized. "They don't know we're on Aelftus soil here. They want her for what? Leverage? But against who?"

A woman stepped timidly from behind the counter with a tray of pastries, her nose wrinkling at the ripe sewage smell of us I knew I wouldn't be able to wash off for weeks. "Um... Councilwoman Riicathi?"

The absurdity of her offering some of the incredibly expensive Elvish pastries that catered to the rich Elf stanners and high society patrons who bought into the popularity of Elves, had me blinking in surprise enough to not correct her that I preferred Renner. It goes to show that different people handle stress in different ways in situations beyond their control. At least by this, it gave her some normalcy and a modicum of control.

I smiled at the young Elf woman and shook my head. "No, but thank you." I motioned her to the others, and she stepped around with the tray. Normally I would have dove on a chance to have one of the pastries here at Jericho's since I've never felt the need to spend forty dollars for a cream puff willingly. They even had a single doughnut hole drizzled with chocolate for budget-conscious people at twenty-five dollars.

My stomach was doing flips at the moment from so many adrenaline dumps in such a short time and even if I did accept the offer, I knew I couldn't keep it down. Some of our group did take one, including Lis, who shrugged at me apologetically. I chuckled internally.

Then I turned to the door when the soldiers called out again, "If you don't hand over Diedra James in thirty seconds, we will enter and take her by force."

Ok now, that was it. I stepped up to the doors and started trying to drag the tables and benches away. Tana and dad moved up to me. "Itty Bit, what are you doing?"

I looked from him to the others. "They know damn well what is really happening here. They're wanting to use her as a tool." Then I said with more conviction and vitriol than I realized I possessed about the past of mom's clan as I added, "The Riicathi won't be used by anyone, ever again."

Dad looked at me long and hard then inclined his head and just started disassembling the barricade with ease, his strength nearly rivaling most full Elves. When Ivan and Pietor started forward to stop us, dad just turned to them. "Either help my daughter or stay back and protect the others."

They glared at each other before Ivan nodded once. "Da." Then he and his brother stood next to Deidre's children.

Looking back one last time as we got a door clear, I said, "Get everyone behind the counter or in the restrooms." Then before anyone could protest I turned to the door and yelled, "I'm coming out to talk. I represent the International Elf Council's Senior Council."

Tana stepped forward with me. I glared at her but she cocked a brow in challenge. I sighed and moved to the door as the man on the bullhorn called out, "This isn't Council business, and you are out of your jurisdiction, you have no authority here. Step outside with your hands where we can see them."

I pulled the door open and we stepped forward with our hands up at our sides, and she noted I stopped with my toes just inside the threshold and she followed suit. I swallowed, trying to hear over the sound of my own heart's hammering.

I channeled Evander Laun as I put on a smirk and said loudly so the men twenty feet away with all the heavy weaponry pointed at us could hear, addressing the man in a generic black suit from one of the alphabet soup of agencies, likely FBI or even Homeland itself. "And that is where you would be wrong. And if you storm this establishment for someone you were just informed was officially given asylum by the International Elf Council... then I'm sure that would break many of the provisions of the Reveal Accords, and be quite probably tantamount to an act of war on Aelftus soil."

The man raised his sidearm toward us as he nudged his chin back toward the towers, smirking, "But you're not on Aelftus soil."

Just then someone called out, "NYPD, lower your weapons." And a harried-looking Detective De Luca stepped up in a line of her boys in blue, all their weapons trained on the soldiers.

The man said, "You're out of your depth, Detective. This is a Homeland Security matter, and you're committing treason by raising your weapons to..."

She cut him off. "One, nobody is buying your bullshit assertion you're from Homeland..." she paused before continuing with a challenge in her eyes, "Major Thorton." His eyes widened slightly in surprise she somehow knew who he was. "And two, we're in contact with the National Guard unit that had been mobilized for this incident, and they were told to stand down by someone in D.C. So these men, are impersonating National Guard soldiers... I hate spooks, and you're not going to pull your off-the-books black ops shit in this town."

He chuckled and made a spreading motion with his hands, his gun lazily flopping with the motion. He didn't even try denying it. He said, "This is above your pay grade, detective, and just one call and people so high above you that would give you a nosebleed just thinking about it will have you and all these officers demoted to meter duty in seconds."

She shrugged. "Then do it. I'm sure Miss Renner here, a
reporter for WTRL News, would be happy to report on this whole
matter. Including that the supposedly 'Died In Action,' Major
Thorton, and the Project Pelican black ops group operating on
American soil. I'm sure your CIA and Congress handlers would
have your hide."

He looked as shocked as me that she knew so much about
them... and my blood ran cold at the mention of Project Pelican.
We learned just recently that that was the name of the black ops
team that Congress was falling over themselves to disavow when
they were brought down creating the same Elf targeting neurotoxin which had nearly killed me a few months back.

Again, he didn't even try to deny it. And I realized this was a
target of opportunity for the group that was supposedly disbanded
but apparently alive and well. They likely saw this as a way to
sow doubt in the population and damage the credibility of the Elf
Council.

The Major shrugged and lazily waved his gun toward me.
"We'll see where the chips fall after we arrest the fugitive and
haul this annoying pointy in for questioning. They are harboring
a non-elf terrorist, and are within the borders of the United States.
So if you and your lackeys here wouldn't mind lowering your..."

My hands were shaking, and not from the adrenaline this time.
There were few times in my life, if any, that I can say I was truly

filled with barely-contained rage. And this asshat just won the lottery. "Again, Major, you are wrong on so many things. Deidre RIICATHI is indeed an Elf, who was helping Elves trapped in a hostile regime to get to safety... an Aelftus matter. And your assertion that we're in the United States? Again, you're in err. It seems being ill-informed is a habit of yours. You... are standing on U.S. Soil out there, and we..." I slid my toe along the threshold of the door, "...are on Aelftus sovereign territory in this Elf-owned building."

He started to talk and I glared at him as I said with acid in my tone, "I am Killishia Renner-Riicathi, a member of the Elf Council's Senior Council, and we voted to give asylum to Deidre Riicathi. All the proper paperwork is filed with the federal government and with the United Nations according to the provisions of the Reveal Accords. So if you..."

I noted a cell phone move up by my cheek, Lisa was there. "...violate any more laws in your attempt to detain an Aelftus citizen, the Council will come down on you like Thor's Hammer with all the political and legal remedies afforded us by those same Accords. And Miss Rodriguez here will stream all of this on so many social media platforms and to WTRL that your computer geeks will never be able to hide all the evidence."

He flinched first, exhaling in exasperation and looking away to the fake National Guard. He spun a finger in the air as he holstered his weapon. "Saddle up. We're heading back to the rally point." And he started to walk away, ignoring all the police weapons trained on them as they all started to load up in their military vehicles.

Sofia called out, "Where do you think you're going? You are all under..."

He called back as he got into a black SUV, "Take the win, De Luca. We'd be out before the doors close behind us at your station." Then to me, as he closed the door, "Next time Riicathi."

I flipped him off and then did a doubletake when I glanced at Tana who was looking at me in... awe? Hunger? As she whispered with a little lust in her tone, "Badass."

I felt ten degrees of bashful as I tucked some hair behind my ear. Then I looked to De Luca who appeared to be two seconds from spitting nails and brimstone. I winged a thumb in the air like I was hitchhiking, "We could use a two-block escort if it isn't too much trouble?" Then I quickly added, "The mercenaries? Was anyone hurt?"

She muttered as she tried to hide a smile, "Nobody but the trail of bodies your group left behind. There were three dozen more found littering a warehouse back there. How did your two bodyguards do all that? Two officers were shot, and are being treated for non-life-threatening gunshot wounds. These ass clowns shot up Manhattan to get to that woman."

I shrugged and told a half-truth, "The Cookie Twins are just very good at their job? It's good that everyone is going to be ok." Then I added, "Do you think Uncle Sam really condones Project Pelican?"

Chapter 14 - Security Session

That's when my grandparents and the rest of the Riicathi arrived on the scene, surprising everyone at their sudden appearance. I was blurting out to Sofia when all the NYPD officers drew on them after a heartbeat of shock, "They're with us! They're... well... they're my family. Riicathi."

De Luca looked from them to me, her own service weapon halfway drawn. "I thought you were the last of the Riicathi, now this woman and all these others?"

"I didn't know myself until today."

Deidre said calmly as the newcomers started to tense, looking ready to explode into action any moment, "Detective? This won't go the way your men think if they get overzealous."

Sofia looked from her to Deidre's children, eyes widening a bit at Jacob before snapping her eyes to mine. Then she scanned the others, her eyes again stopping on the other Halfling. "Stand down, men."

Just an hour later we were up in the suite of rooms just below the Penthouses in Laun Tower that were normally used for visiting dignitaries and their entourages when they come to speak with the International Elf Council. They were the rooms Evander and Marcillia had the staff set up for Deidre and her family, and the rest of the floor was now filled with Riicathi.

Marcillia looked to be amazed as she watched them all as they were shown their rooms. "There are so many. The Riicathi thrive."

I was just nodding, pride swelling in my chest for the clan I had only learned I was part of a few short months ago. "Isn't it wonderful?"

She said with sincerity, punctuating to me the fact that the guilt and desire to attempt to somehow make amends with my clan who was treated so reprehensibly, used as nothing but blunt instruments, had hope of being attainable, "It truly is, Killishia."

Then her brow furrowed as she took in a few of the people milling about, "Is there a senior member of the Riicathi that will be taking your seat on the..."

Deidre and a silver haired Elf she was speaking with named Tomas, turned and shook their heads, Deidre stating firmly, "No." And Tomas just inclining his head to me, "Killishia Abigail Renner-Riicathi has led the revival of the Riicathi well, as Minya. The rest of us have watched from afar when the rumors began that a Riicathi had emerged and was given a seat on the Council, signifying the Riicathi were free. And none of us could have hoped to make such sweeping changes for not only our clan, but for all Aelftus kind as she has."

Tomas echoed Deidre, "No. If our eldest, Audrey and Emit Riicathi defer to their granddaughter, the rest of us would be fools not to." Then he looked back at me and inclined his head again, "Minya."

I was just blinking. I had only heard Evander Laun or Natalia Havashire ever referred to as Minya, meaning 'The First' in old Aelftus. It seemed almost ludicrous that they would call me that. Or that with all the other more senior Riicathi now revealed, that they would even want me leading them.

Mom had joined us, her first time ever in Laun Tower as she has stayed as far away from the Council as she could, even after we became equals to the other clans with our voting share of the Míre. The news of so many more of our people was too much temptation for her to ignore. She reached over and closed my mouth which had been hanging open as I tried to process everything. "That's a good way to catch flies, sweetheart."

Natalia Havashire, who was pinching the bridge of her nose at the door of the main suite, said to herself distractedly, "More Halflings. And the protesters saw them on the street when they were brought in. Videos are already showing up online." She glanced over almost accusingly toward Lisa, who was just one of the three Sapiens ever allowed on these upper floors, besides dad and now Detective De Luca, who weren't leaders of various nations.

I knew for a fact Lis hadn't posted any of her footage yet, and wouldn't until I said it would be ok. She knew how volatile and explosive the revelation that the two sub-species of Human can interbreed was going to be.

Pursing my lips and squinting an eye in mock pain I asked, "How is the Council going to spin this?"

Dimitri responded, "I don't think it can be hidden any longer. With you it was possible because you have mostly manifested Elvish features, but it is clear that these other two display undeniable Sapien traits." He was looking past me to Jacob's ears and just shook his head slowly, though his eyes reflected amazement instead of judgment.

Lisa asked the question I had been thinking again, "Is there something different about the Riicathi that make it more possible for interbreeding of Human branches?"

I turned to the Senior members and added to that, "What clans did the first two Halfling babies in the past hail from?" I was seriously curious what the answer was even though I'm sure they heard the last of the thought, 'which you had the Riicathi Pallbearers dispatch.'

Evander answered, sounding curious himself, "Claude would have that answer. What we do know is that there have been dozens of other pregnancies over the centuries, even one reported just forty years ago right here in New York, but in all cases, either the mother and child died in childbirth or the children were stillborn."

It was such a tragedy that something that should be a joyous occasion, something created in love, was akin to a death sentence. Marcillia sharing, "Which is why all Aelftus are discouraged from intimate relations with Sapiens." She glanced Lisa's way.

That was something I didn't know. I thought it was looked down upon because most Elves looked down on Sapiens as distasteful, I always wrote it off as entitled arrogance that the Aelftus thought we were superior to Sapiens. I guess I had to rethink my own misconception a little now. Frack, personal growth makes me itch.

Lisa mumbled to herself, "Noted."

Then Marcillia added on the prior line of thinking, "The medical staff theorize the Riicathi are the next evolution of Aelftus, with their ability to regulate the Protoelastin in their blood, and have quicker reflexes and are more... durable. Perhaps it is these differences, and that durability of the Riicathi which affords you more likely to survive Halfling childbirth?"

Natalia exhaled, looking contemplative as she prompted everyone, "That is a question for another time, right now, we need to convene the Emergency Security Session, to address the attack on Aelftus citizens in an attempt to assassinate one of our own."

She cocked her head slightly and asked Deidre, "Will you stand in the Chamber to give your eyewitness testimony, and address the revelation of more Aelftus families in Ethiopia, and their current dispositions after the raid?"

Deidre nodded slowly, "Of course. And once the heat has died down some, I'll be heading back to free those I can if any are left alive, if you can ensure my children's safety here before I go."

Mercy and Charity stepped forward, looking fierce and defiant, Mercy almost accusing, "Mother, we are going with..."

"No, you are not. They have no doubt figured out I wasn't alone, and why I appeared to be in multiple places at once. Your safety is my number one priority as your mother. I should never have trained you in the Riicathi ways."

"But, mother..."

I took a step forward and Evander held up a halting hand to everyone, "One thing at a time. Now that we are aware of our people's plight there, the Council will have something to say about it."

Then to me, his wife, and his Havashire counterparts, he said with steel in his tone, "Shall we?"

We all nodded, and Tana looped one arm in mine and one in Deidre's, I took one last look at the Riicathi moving about in the hall, amazed that even with all the violence, besides some scrapes and bruises, there was only one serious injury. Though one tall woman had taken a bullet to the shoulder, and the Elf was down in the medical sub-level now, our doctors seeing to her injury.

A woman stepped up and held out two phones to Tana, saying, "Cloned your old phones as requested, Aryon." Tana inclined her head in thanks and the woman scurried off, looking like she were trying to make herself as small as possible so the high ranking Elves around here wouldn't take notice. Then my girl handed me a duplicate of my old LaunPhone, complete with Firefly Serenity case. I blinked and unlocked it to see all my apps and contacts were there. They had cloned the information from my phone? That is some spooky butt Big Brother mojo right there.

Then we were heading to the elevator, dad reaching out as we passed to give my shoulder an encouraging squeeze, and mom resting a hand momentarily on my arm, giving me a proud yet mischievous look that had Tanny blurting out, "I swear to God, if you tell us to have fun storming the castle, I'm going to scream, Abigail."

Mom scrunched up her face and asked me, "This one is no fun, you sure she's the one?"

I sighed heavily and dragged the women on as I whined out, "Mooom."

De Luca was calling out, "God damn it Renner, I need to get statements from all of you before I leave this shit show to those over my pay-grade." I just waved awkwardly behind me, causing her to growl.

A minute later we were down in the Council Chamber, the corridor twice as busy as before if that was possible. And a lot more wicked looking automatic rifles and security keeping everyone back from the huge Chamber doors.

My cell buzzed and I glanced down at it before the signal was blocked when they engage the white noise curtain and electronic jammers. I had to double take. It was Hansa Susanti, the ambassador to the Dearmadta, and primary contact for them in the Riicathi Consortium I had set up by the legal pool to give the Dearmadta a say in critical Council votes that would affect them, giving them a voice in matters they had no control of before.

The message was terse and I winced seeing three other texts from her still unanswered. She was wanting to know what was going on here since reports were coming in all around the world and videos were popping up online. I quickly shot off, "I'll call you as soon as the Emergency Security Session is over. I promise."

This seemed to placate her as she responded simply with, "I will await your call." My life couldn't be any more hectic than it was right now, and everyone wanted answers, some of which I couldn't give since I was in the dark just as much as them.

I looked to Claude, sitting at his secretary desk just inside the doors, and I sent him a quick text too. He looked at his cell then up to me as I crossed the Chamber with Deidre and Tana, then looked down, squinting through his ultra-thick glasses as he sent back, "The first record doesn't list a clan. As for the one which had the Riicathi rebelling then fleeing to the New World?"

There was a long pause before he sent, "Riicathi." I spun back to look at him, his eyes filled with sorrow and... well and rage. He made no secret that he wholeheartedly condemned the Council for their decisions back then... him being only one of two Elves still alive from that time, three hundred years ago.

Fut the actual wuck? That ancient Council almost wiped out my clan, then forced the last handful to kill some of our own? Ok, now I was understanding more, the rage I saw in the faces of most of the newfound Riicathi whenever the Council was brought up.

Turning to look around at the current Council, I knew I couldn't be mad at them for something prior generations did, so I swallowed my anger at people long dead and concentrated on what was happening now. There were still Elves in a dire situation, though I didn't know what we could do about it. And Deidre running off on her own, right back into danger for others, seemed wrong to me.

I reached my seat, but looked around, feeling it wouldn't be right to take the seat with Deidre behind me in the risers, so instead I stood in front of the railing around my seat with Tana and Deidre at my side. I felt, I don't know, inadequate next to my cousin as she radiated a confidence I was a little envious of. Tanny was getting to know me better than I knew myself at times, and slipped her hand in mine to give it a reassuring squeeze.

People were covering their noses, reminding me we hadn't had a chance to clean up yet, and my feet were still damp with things I didn't want to contemplate from our sewer run.

There were whispers that everyone could hear circulating, speculating about who this outsider was in the Chamber where only Council Members and security were allowed. I noted Issac's parents looking my way inquisitively, concern on their faces. Had Issac not had a moment to inform them he was ok yet? I mouthed to them, "He's fine." His mother visibly relaxed, exhaling long and hard, her shoulders slumping slightly. This just affirmed to me the worry all mothers had for their children.

Even Marcillia had looked Tana over when we first arrived at the Tower, concern creasing the corners of her eyes, causing my girl to whisper, "Mooom, stop. I'm fine."

Evander, from his seat in the middle of the upper right risers, motioned to the door, and to my surprise, eight security personnel, and the Cookie Twins moved inside before Claude closed the door. I could see all the security types physically stopping themselves from helping the ancient Elf as he shuffled and creaked his way to the controls, closing the doors, and activating the white noise curtain.

It was still an interesting quirk of Elvish society, how much they revered, respected, and loved the eldest of us. I bit the inside of my cheek to stop from chuckling when they all looked just moments from cheering him on as they watched with bated breath while he turned, seemed to get confused, then looked back at the door again, before seeming to remember and he made his way back to his chair behind that antique secretary desk. They all leaned forward, as if they could assist with their thought as he prepared himself then sat down. I knew the only thing he wasn't faking was the creaking of his bones and tendons as he sat and settled in the chair.

He paused and looked around the Chamber, re-centering his thick glasses on his nose. "Oh, hello."

Natalia called down to him from the Havashire's side of the Chamber. "Hello, Claude, dear." Then she tapped her gavel. "This Emergency Security Session of the International Elf Council is now convened. I'm sure all of you already know why we called this session, as it is all over the news. But first, I'd like to introduce the new face in the Chamber beside Killishia Renner-Riicathi. This Elf is from a newly discovered branch of the Riicathi clan. The Ethiopian military government knows her as Deidre James, but she is Deidre Riicathi."

There were gasps and murmurs, and my ears swiveled back to that familiar voice which seemed to always be heckling me in the

Chamber, who muttered, "Just great, there's more of her." I looked back to see who spoke but like always, it wasn't apparent who the speaker was.

Deidre just took a single step forward and inclined her head slightly to each side of the aisle then to the non-voting members seated behind us before stepping back to my side.

Then the Launs and Havashires alternated in recounting the harrowing extraction of Deidre and her family, and went into graphic detail of the assassination attempt and the arrival of the rest of the Riicathi clan. Of the fact there was a leak somewhere along the line, whether from inside the Council, or the NYPD, since the bounty hunting mercenaries, and Ethiopian soldiers had been laying in wait.

Then they detailed the involvement of the fake National Guard unit made of a Project Pelican team and my idea to get to Aelftus soil in the bakery, and finally our arrival here at the sanctuary of Laun Tower.

So Evander ended with, "So it seems we have four security concerns here before us today which the Council must act upon. First and foremost is the fact that contrary to all assertions by the Laramer Bloc nations, it has come to light that there are still Aelftus citizens trapped in those zero tolerance, anti-Elf nations, and we cannot allow that to stand. Elves help Elves, it is our creed, and it is how we've survived for eons beside the Sapiens."

Then he looked over to us, "Deidre, would you please address the Council about how you came about intelligence of the possibility of Aelftus families hiding away in Ethiopia, and your efforts to get them to safety? And what you witnessed while in no-man's land as you are the only known Elf to have infiltrated a Laramer Bloc country."

She took a deep breath as he motioned to the podium set up in the middle of the Chamber, between the two sides, then she nodded, straightened her bloodied shirt, then strode out with the fluid grace of a predator.

She leaned on the podium, bracing her hands against it as she leaned slightly in to the microphone, even though it was unnecessary in a room full of people who could hear the slightest whisper. I've always contemplated the microphone myself, and all I could think of is that it's probable the proceedings were recorded for the official record.

"Hello, as has been shared, I am Deidre, great granddaughter of Remus Riicathi." This got some gasps from a few people, telling me some of those gathered were familiar with the true history of the Pallbearers, one was Natalia herself who was well versed in our plight. I noted Claude's eyes go wide as he seemed to stop himself from standing.

I absently wondered why it was so shocking, besides the fact that more Riicathi yet lived. Romulus Riicathi was my great great grandfather after all.

She looked from one side to the other, and even though she had to be a bundle of nervous apprehension, being in the Chamber of the Council the Riicathi have been running from for the last three centuries, she leaned in again and stated, "I cannot share where my intelligence originated from, but can assure you it is from the most trusted of sources the Riicathi have. Nor can I divulge the network used to spirit the trapped Elves from Ethiopian territory."

There were some murmurs as she spoke over them, "But I can confirm that there were over two hundred and fifty Elves hiding from the illegitimate military rulers there. Our efforts were able to get over two hundred souls to safety of countries beyond Laramer Bloc borders."

She took a deep breath and centered herself, looking back at me for a moment before continuing, "I will disclose the atrocities I witnessed, or those trapped there shared with me, including the public executions of any Elves or suspected Elves the government there has found since their coup after the Reveal."

She clenched a fist and almost growled out, "And I can tell you of the raid that occurred while we attempted to get the last to safety after our location was leaked to the military. And how they killed or captured all the Elves or suspected Elves as I made my escape, much to my own shame."

I noted she didn't bring up that her daughters had been with her there, even though the Launs and Havshires knew. I understood, she was protecting her children, and there was a mole either in the Council, or the NYPD and she was taking no chances.

She turned around slowly, taking everyone in, verifying she had their undivided attention. "Even though they still think I'm Sapien, the true reason they are so adamant about finding me and having me extradited to their country, and why they sent mercenaries and their own soldiers to New York to assassinate me, is not that I'm as they say, an Elf sympathizer, but that they want to silence me before I can share what I have witnessed of their Aelftus genocide, of which I have video proof."

"So even though I have no great love for the International Elf Council, I will share all and hope that my Minya, Killishia," she motioned my way, "is correct in her assertions that this is a different Council than that which enslaved our people so long ago."

This got some angry exclamations from some, and thoughtful and embarrassed looks from others, causing Dimitri to pound his gavel for silence. Then we all just sat there, entranced by the horrific tale she shared in so much more detail than she had with me. And by the time she was wrapping it up, I was wiping tears from my face, my heart feeling an odd mix of crushing sorrow and a burning need to hold the Laramer Bloc accountable for the atrocities she shared in such vivid detail.

The image that was stuck in my head was when she shared that they had a Elf body which was nothing but rags and bone now, displayed in front of their military capitol building as a trophy and warning to others to what would happen to any Elves or sympathizers caught within the country.

As I looked around, every Elf, to a one, had similar appalled and determined looks on their faces.

Diedre just stared at the microphone a moment, her eyes unfocused before she stood tall, and straightened her shirt again in that nervous habit, and she marched right back to Tana and me and stood beside us, chin high in defiance.

Chapter 15 – Vote

I was so very not qualified for the literal decisions that were before us, nor did I feel equipped to handle important things which had ramifications having a high probability of shaking the foundation of the United Nations and all the other signatories of the Reveal Accords. But who was?

When prompted, Deidre went to the podium again and produced a memory device from a pocket. A projection screen lowered a few feet in front of the Chamber doors when she inserted the memory device in the computer at the base of the podium and we watched the unthinkable. The execution of Elves... men, women, children.

In one video, the illegitimate leader of the Ethiopian regime himself took a gun from one of his men in a raid to shoot an Elvish woman in the head. Having many of us gasping at the inhumanity and almost glee his men had as they killed surrendering Elves indiscriminately. Only after most were lying dead did they stop shooting and beat and dragged away the few they left alive.

I wiped the tears from my eyes that had blurred my vision onto my sleeve. This was something that would haunt me the rest of my days, and I felt a scar on my heart. Did the international community know about this? Or was the country so sealed off their anti-Elf rhetoric was seen as just saber rattling?

Then still pictures of other atrocities from contacts who had got them to Deidre through private channels, as well as official military documents with the state seal, in what I assumed was Oromo, the main language of Ethiopia, She shared that they were official shoot on sight orders for not just Elves, but for any "human" aiding them... Elf sympathizers.

Then she pulled the device back out of the computer and the screen retraced back into the ceiling, leaving the entire Chamber in shocked and appalled silence.

Evander straightened his tie, as if it were uncomfortably tight, and tapped his gavel lightly in the quiet of the Chamber, and said in a slightly hoarse tone. "We will now vote on condemning Ethiopia and the Laramer Bloc for the atrocities that have been perpetrated against Aelftus citizens. And issuing a formal claim of breach of International Law and genocide against the sitting Ethiopian government, as well as an arrest warrant for the General Yafet Yohannes, the leader of the Ethiopian Military Authority Defense Force for murder."

Natalia looked around and asked, "Those in favor?"

There was a somber chorus of, "Aye," my voice sounding so very small in the mix.

"Those opposed," was met with a cold silence. She tapped her gavel. "Let the record show the unanimous passing of this issue. Please send in the representative from legal."

One of the guards opened the door, and a silver haired, impeccably dressed man strode in... he must have been waiting for this. It was Mr. Muhammad, Aldrich's boss. The seriousness of the situation was punctuated by his presence in the Chamber.

Once the doors were closed on the crowd of Elves looking through them, Dimitri spoke to him as he stopped at the podium, "Salman, Deidre has evidence of Aelftus genocide that will need to be disseminated to the Untied Nations, the World Court, and the signatories of the Accords along with our condemnation of their actions." The man inclined his head as Deidre hesitantly strode out yet again to the middle to hand it to the lawyer.

Marcillia added, "We need formal murder charges and extradition requests drawn up for General Yohannes, it will be obvious when you review the evidence."

He looked from one side to the other and inclined his head again, "Yes Minyas, right away."

Evander told him, "Please stay, Salman. There is more business..."

"Of course, Minya."

He stood with his hands behind his back, looking as immensely competent as the few times I ever saw him down in the legal department.

Marcillia looked around, and her voice was still colored by what we witnessed, "As you all know, as a sovereign people pursuant to the Accords, we are a permanent member of the United Nations and NATO as a landless nation. The next order of business is possibly the most important vote we of the International Elf Council have ever had to consider, as it will affect us in the most profound manner since the Reveal itself."

She looked our way, "Tanaliashia, please set the Chair of the Riicathi's phone to bypass the Chamber jamming. The seriousness of this decision will impact all Aelftus, not just the voting houses, as the representative for the Dearmadta, Miss Renner will need to cast her next vote through the Riicathi Consortium."

Tana looked from her mother to me then back again, then with her cheeks heating, she put her hand out to me and I handed her my LaunPhone. She somehow pulled up what looked like base-code for the operating system and with a few keystrokes, I had full bars again. I blinked and and took in her embarrassment. I knew she could spoof her location with her own hacks, and outside of the Chamber could get past the other jammers, but inside the Chamber too? This was a new level of badassery from my girl that had me cocking a brow.

And Marcillia had known her daughter had that particular skill. Then her mother addressed me, "Killishia, please relay this to Miss Susanti if you would." I nodded slowly and started texting Hansa a quick heads up of what had transpired so far. I just hoped she'd be awake to respond, Thailand was half a world away after all.

Then Dimitri inhaled deeply, held his breath for three heartbeats before stating with iron in his tone, "This genocide of Aelftus citizens amounts to an act of war against our people and our sovereignty, and we cannot let this stand. Those in favor of the Aelftus' official stance that war has been declared upon us, and we reserve the right to respond in an appropriate manner in which to ensure this won't occur again, whether that response be diplomatic, heavy sanctions, or militarily, or calling upon allied nations from the United Nations and NATO to back us in our response."

There was a long delay, the silence seemed to be swallowing the world, the only sound to my embarrassment was the little ticking sound from my cell as my fingers flew across the keys as I texted Hansa furiously, before the first person was saying "Aye," then more followed until it was a chorus of "Aye"s.

Then all eyes were on me, and I wanted to shrink away as seconds ticked by, then a single word appeared on my screen from Hansa, who was awake and had seen my texts. I straightened, a lump in my throat as I held my chin up, willing my voice not to waver as I stated, "The Ricathii Consortium votes aye."

Satisfied, she looked around. "Opposed?"

Two dissenting, "Nay"s called out. And nobody even looked for them, because a lot of us were on the fence here... we were basically acknowledging that we saw the Ethiopian actions as a declaration of war, and war was a frightening thing, especially since a lot of the governments out there were still uneasy about Elves, the USA included with groups like Project Pelican being run off the books. We couldn't blame the dissenters for not wanting that kind of attention on us and not wanting war.

Then one voice called out, "Abstain."

Dimitri called out, "Let the record show that the Aye's have it by the required super-majority required for this vote."

I wondered what that would look like if we truly did go to war, but then I remembered the majority of the military weapons and equipment in the world were produced by Aelftus owned companies. Is this why? Had they anticipated that one day, we may need to defend ourselves from our fellow humans? I didn't wish to ponder that any more.

Natalia looked down to Mr. Muhammad, "Salman?"

The lawyer, whose color had drained from his face inclined his head, "Yes Minya, all the communiques will be sent."

Evander added, "We'll need formal paperwork demanding the release of any Elves held in captivity, or still in hiding in Ethiopia AND the Larmaner Bloc."

Deidre barked out with venom, "Paperwork? Paperwork? Elves are dying. I intend on infiltrating the country again and freeing as many of our people as I can while the Council... wallows in bureaucracy while people are dying!"

It was Natalia Havashire standing and walking down the risers to the floor of the Chamber and walking right up to us to clasp one of my cousin's hands between her own, "I know your pain and rage, Deidre, but we aren't just going to be sitting idly by while Elves are dying. We have to make our intentions known for the international community, doing things right while we put together a strike team from our own security force and hopefully our allies as the defense treaties dictate."

Then with fire and venom as she looked toward the southeast, her voice as hard as cold steel, "Then we are going in there en force with you to free our people, and investigate the other Bloc countries for any of our people who were left behind. Know that the Riicathi no longer have to stand alone."

A rumble of, "Here here," came from the Council members.

My cousin exhaled, deflated, then smirked, "That was pretty good. Don't make me like you, Havashire."

Natalia smirked right back. Then the smirks faded from their faces as the seriousness of the situation reasserted itself. It was time for the Elves to go to war, and it scared me to death.

Evander called out, "And now for the next order of business." He looked down at the lawyer and said, "Salman, I'm sure you already anticipated our prior votes and likely already had the paperwork ready to send. But given new evidence provided to us by Mrs. Riicathi, we'll need a separate set of formal paperwork demanding the release and repatriation of any Aelftus remains in Ethiopia AND the Larmaner Bloc, including the corpse on display at their military capitol building... this is to have the highest priority. The victims need to be identified and maybe we can provide some closure for their families if they can be located. There are some pictures in evidence on the device."

Instead of calling for a vote on it, he just looked around the Chamber, a hand held out palm up, inviting any challenge. There was none, as people were just nodding. I can't imagine how the families of the victims have been feeling, not knowing the fates of family members who didn't get out of the Bloc counties before borders were sealed. It would be a cold comfort knowing for certain, but better than always wondering and imagining the worst anyway.

Mr. Muhammad said in a somber tone, "Yes, Minya. Of course."

Evander inclined his head. "Thank you Salman, that will be all." And with the grace and efficiency, the lawyer took powerful strides indicative of Elves to the doors, then exited, the guards sealing the doors behind him.

With that, the two Senior families seemed to relax and decompress into their seats, Marcillia rubbing her face, looking weary from the weight of the actions we had all just set in motion.

Natalia however smiled over at me with a resigned and patient grin, "And now that the ball is set in motion on that nasty mess, it seems that we have another whole other unraveling ball of yarn on our hands. Courtesy of young Killishia's family, imagine that." Her grin was a full on smile now as chuckles circulated through the risers.

I tried not to whine as I whined out, "I'm not that bad." Another round of chuckles rippled through the Chamber. I huffed out to everyone, "Whatever." Why did I have a feeling I knew what this particular ball of yarn was she was intimating, and it wasn't my motion to restore the voting shares and dissolve all proxy contracts. No that was still a whole other mess... well, ok, maybe I rock the boat on occasion, but I wasn't that bad, was I?

Dimitri looked at his wife patiently for baiting me, and the man winked down at me and then addressed the Chamber. "This assassination attempt has brought to light a... situation that the Launs and we Havashires have been putting off until a good time in our relations with our allies were stronger, but now there's nothing for it. The genie is out of the bottle, as it were, and we can't just stuff it back in now."

He looked around the Chamber slowly, seeing all eyes focused on him as he appeared to be searching for the proper words. He settled for, "Miss Renner, if you would be so kind." He motioned toward the podium.

Oh great, I felt like a lab rat a teacher was putting on display for their students. I started walking on reflex, tripping on what must have been a really tough molecule of air, or possibly nothing at all. I spun low to absorb the kinetic energy of the fall, and stopped back to back with one of the big security guards... well big is relative since almost everyone was big to me, but the man wasn't as big as the Cookie Twins by far.

I had managed to stop leaving a hair's breath of space between us before I dropped my head and shuffled over to the podium. I kept my eyes down as my cheeks and neck heated from the embarrassment. When I glanced back, Deidre was grinning warmly with a glint of recognition in her eye at my clumsiness.

Natalia stood from her seat. "Some of you have already surmised what we are about to share with you, but recent events have forced an accelerated timetable for sharing it with the rest of you and the world. Pictures have been flooding the Internet in the past couple hours and we need to make an official announcement to stay ahead of it to keep any panic to a minimum."

"I know we have told the media and the members of the Elf Council here, that Killishia's... eccentricities... her eye color, and her adorable little ears were defects from a complicated birth. And we've shared with the press that there are other Elves with various eye colors, but the dominant color is blue."

I bristled at the word defects again. I wasn't defective, I was just me.

She sighed heavily and motioned a hand down to me, "Young Kia is actually the offspring of a Sapien and Aelftus... a Halfling."

This elicited a gasp from around half of the Chamber, which told me Natalia was right, quite few had already surmised my situation already. The Dearmadta had known the second they saw me, so I guess it wasn't as big a secret as we thought.

Marcillia said from the other side of the aisle, "As you know, our relations with our host country here, the United States is tenuous at best. And we need to address Congress again about their supposed investigation into Project Pelican as it just came to light that they are still there, and well funded. Knowledge of the possibility of Sapien and Aelftus offspring, while likely to be celebrated by some of the population, may cause panic in others. It was this panic which we had been avoiding."

She pinched the bridge of her nose, "But in this age of information, where everyone has a camera in the palm of their hands, we can't stop what is coming after today. Images of two other Halflings with prominent Sapien traits who arrived with the Riicathi strike team that allowed Deidre to get here, are already circulating with speculation as to their disposition. We can't hide it from the public anymore. All we can do is damage control and hope it doesn't spiral out of control."

I noted how she didn't reveal one was Deidre's son. Was it on purpose, was she still concerned about the leak possibly being on the Council side?

"So now it isn't an if or when, it is a here and now. We need to get ahead of this before the press runs rampant with theories. We propose basically a second Reveal, pointing out the reason we didn't share right away was because we thought Killishia was the only one."

I could feel all eyes on me and I was wondering if I could spontaneously turn invisible if I really really wanted it... nope, apparently not. Evander spoke in an almost kind and sympathetic tone, "We think Miss Renner herself can be our point person on this as she has already made a name for herself on her WTRL segment that has been swinging popular opinion toward the Aelftus."

Then he said directly to me, "Since this is a topic you are intimately familiar with, the Senior Council leaves the announcement and manner of disclosure in your hands, Kia. The sooner the better before too many alternate theories start running rampant out there."

I swallowed hard as my ears started swiveling everywhere as the chaos I was starting to equate to me here in the Chamber erupted around us. So many people shouting questions to the senior families and to me. Protests and concerns and even encouragements.

Evander pounded his gavel. "Order! We will have order in the Chamber!" Dimitri and Natalia's gavels joined in, the sharp cracks sounding over the cacophony of voices which were only gaining volume.

Seriously now, just eff my life.

Chapter 16 - WTRL

That... is how we wound up here, back at the station just a couple hours later, after we had a chance to get out of our sewage soaked clothing and get cleaned up. I called Tobias Klien as Tana, Lisa and I loaded up in the Cookie Twins' replacement SUV. Surprised we had an escort of seven vehicles with heavily armed Elves this time, and a helicopter flying above us with men hanging out the doors with automatic weapons.

I prompted Ivan, who sat in the back with us as Pietor drove, "Overkill much?"

He said in a matter of fact tone, "Da, we were just attacked using a garbage truck just hours ago, do you not remember Miss Kia?"

Lisa said brightly, "That's true."

Sighing I prompted as I hung my head to place in my hands, "They were trying to assassinate Deidre, they weren't after me."

Tana offered helpfully almost before I was done speaking, "This time."

"Right, this... hey! You're supposed to be on my side."

"You can't blame them for tightening security, I mean, if you weren't so unimaginably fast, you could have been hurt or worse, Killy." Then she motioned toward the street as we moved through the last vestiges of rush hour traffic, the sun having set just minutes before. "And now you're going to make an announcement almost as world changing as the Reveal was. So it would be nice if you had support if things go all pear shaped when that occurs, and they can get you to safety."

Again I sighed and looked though the windshield to the three diplomatic flags fastened to the sides of the hood. The U.S. Flag, the United Nations Flag, and the flag of the Aelftus nation. "Yes, I understand, but seven vehicles plus a six car police escort?"

She said with smirk, "At least we put your detective to good use."

My cheeks heated and I tucked an unruly red strand of hair behind my ear. Detective De Luca seemed to be the only thing that ruffled my girl's feathers, she was always so confident and I thought her jealousy was sort of adorable as it showed she was human like everyone else. "She's not my detective, woman."

Lisa was of no help at all as she asked with bright eyes, "Ooo, Detective Hottie? She almost does it for me too."

"Not helping, Lis."

"Helping wasn't my intention, Kia." Then she changed the topic, "You didn't say how Mr. Klien reacted to your request."

It was my turn to brighten. "Well when I told him I'd finally agree to the interview he has been pushing me for since I Elfed, he sounded overjoyed, I think he was imagining another Peabody.

But when I told him it was under a few conditions, he was a little less enthusiastic."

Tana asked, "What conditions?"

"Well for one, I wanted him doing the interview, not our prime-time host, Mary. He agreed readily. Then I told him that this one needed to be shared fully with ENN since they had global reach instead of just the New York area. That was a tougher sell. Then my final condition was that he could only ask five questions after I made an announcement that was going to change how the general public viewed us Elves."

Lis was nodding. "Yup, that'd do it."

After the short, roundabout ride, which avoided the three blocks along the route we had taken as we fled toward the safety of Laun Tower, which was mostly blocked by NYPD vehicles and police tape, we drove past the station slowly.

Some of the our vehicles stopping at the underground parking entrance while the rest of the convoy continued on around the block before the all clear was given over the radio. I won't admit to flinching a little every time we passed alleyways during the drive. The memory of the chaotic seconds that followed the garbage truck plowing into us was still too fresh in my mind.

Then we pulled up to the front doors, the police and Aelftus Security forming lines holding the foot traffic and a small gathering crowd of what appeared to be Elf Stanners back. This seemed overkill to me. It was almost as overboard as the security for the Transparency Conference had been in Bangkok.

We stopped at the curb and waited five heartbeats as my Russian protectors scanned the crowd until a barely audible, "Clear," was heard on Ivan's earpiece.

He looked at the three of us. "Miss Kia, you and the Aryon will exit the vehicle last, and do exactly as we say."

I swallowed and nodded, which satisfied the big man. He opened the door and stood up on the sidewalk, looked around again, eyes sweeping for threats, then he nodded once. Pietor left the vehicle running and slipped out the driver's door, to walk around to stand on the other side of our door from Ivan.

I jumped a little when an Elf in an impeccably fit suit, silently slipped into the driver's seat and closed the door. Then Ivan called out, "Ladies, if you would, please."

Lisa shrugged at us, but I could see the apprehension she was trying to hide, in her eyes. Then Tana went, holding a hand out for me to take, and she helped me out. The moment we were standing, Ivan had an arm over my shoulders, leading me along the corridor of guards, Pietor doing the same with Tana, keeping Lisa between the two of us as they ushered us to the main doors. People were calling out questions as some of the stanners were calling out, "There's Killishia!" My eyes were assaulted by flashes from cell phone cameras that felt like little ice picks to the front of my brain where another migraine was building.

We were rushed inside where station security and a couple police officers were waiting. I chuckled at the other woman next to them, looking all kinds of dangerous at the moment. "Hello Sofia."

"I'm really starting to hate you, Renner."

I assured the detective, "I'm an acquired taste."

"Miss Laun, Miss Rodriguez."

Lis was all grins as she half saluted, "Detective De Luca." While my girl just eyed her, tilting her chin up slightly. I caught a glimpse of the sinfully soft blood red layer of hair Tana had under her ebony locks which I loved running my fingers through. She's been growing her hair out ever since I mentioned how I liked her long hair in the back. It made me feel a bit bashful knowing she was growing it out for me. The shaved sides she used to sport were almost two inches long now, three months seemed pretty fast growth to me, was it an Elf thing?

Then Sofia prompted, "We've got uniforms stationed at all the exits. Just what is this all about that you need so much security? We've apprehended the gunmen, mercenaries, and Ethiopian Security Services soldiers... the ones left alive or unconscious. We really need to get your security team in to make a statement. And just how did two men take on over three dozen shooters?"

Ivan and Pietor were silent at that, then I squinted an eye in mock pain, really hating to do this because I hated when the Council did it to me. "I'm sorry, but you'll have to go through Council legal for any statements." Then before she could go off on me I shared, "What I'm about to do on air tonight is likely to make things go sideways. So it would be appreciated if your officers can stay until we find out how the public is going to react."

As her brow furrowed, she looked torn between concern and irritation as she shared one of my old goto lines, half in humor, half in that annoyance, "Fucking Elf Accords."

I held up a finger and said succinctly, "Precisely. Sorry."

She rolled a shoulder as she put a hand on it, had she been injured today? And she was still running the assignment?

"Fine, you best be to it then. Most of my team is done with this clusterfuck of a day."

"Them and me both. I just want to go home."

Tanny said as she pulled me along toward Tobias, "Goodbye Detective."

I cocked a brow in challenge to my girl and her emotionless mask broke into a sheepish grin. "Shut up, Killy." I laid my head on her shoulder as we stopped in front of the station manager.

"Hi, Tobias."

With an exhalation of breath he said, "So tell me why I'm not at home right now, with a beer in hand, watching the Syracuse game, Kia?"

"I already told you. The interview you've been..."

"Gah, whatever, Renner. Let's go get you mic-ed up. Rodriguez, make yourself useful and escort Miss Laun and umm... her escorts to the observation room."

When the Cookie Twins started to flank us as Mr. Klien led me away, I pulled us to a stop. "Guys, really, I'll be fine. It'll just be me, Tobias, and the cameraman." I hesitated, "Speaking of, once Lisa's footage of the incident this afternoon is vetted by Council's legal team, she had some phenomenal footage of the attack and subsequent showdown, sir."

Before he could speak, Ivan responded with a firm, "Nyet." I sighed and deflated as the glares the boys were directing at the approaching station security guards, had the Sapien men hesitating and swallowing.

Mr. Klien waved them off, "It's alright Gomez and Williams. Just check on the others while we are in the newsroom." Then nodded and headed off toward the loading dock area in the back.

Seconds later I was in the familiar backstage area partitioned off in the newsroom where Jenicia usually did my makeup and hair for the twice a week segment I was sort of guilted into doing after I Elfed, since WTRL is the only news agency who can tout an on air Elf personality outside of Elf Network News. ENN was one of the many businesses the Jerichos, the third most powerful Elf house, behind the Launs and Havashires, ran.

As I was about to ask where Jenicia was, I stopped in my tracks, blinking... in the room was a tall, impossibly beautiful Elf. Lorenzo Vasquez, the lead anchor for the World Beat news segment of ENN was there in all his two thousand dollar, form fitting suit glory, along with two other Elves, one with camera gear and a woman who had to be his producer judging by the clipboard and tablet she held in the crook of one arm.

My mouth worked without any sound coming out, making me wonder if my verbal circuitry had shorted out. I squeak finally, "You're Lorenzo Vasquez."

He just smiled hugely, showing his perfect teeth, his dark eyes under his expertly tossled black curls were locked on mine as he seemed to be... ah, my green eyes. His rich baritone with the slight Spanish accent and precise diction was just as he sounded on air. "And you, my dear," he grasped my hand between his and shook once then lifted it half way to his mouth in a mock kiss of the back of my hand, "are Killishia Riicathi. We've been sending messages for months to get you on the show."

I shrugged as he released my hand. "Yeaaaah, I ran out of ways to say no."

He chuckled, "And yet, here we are today." He looked
sideways at Tobias and said carefully, "After such an eventful
day."

I nodded and Mr. Klein stated, "And yet here we all are."
Then he leaned into share with possibly the most recognizable
news anchor in the world, "I'm her boss, yet this is the first time
she's agreed to be interviewed for the very station she is
employed at."

They shared a look. What? Boys, men are all boys!

Then Mr. Klein looked past us to the door behind the
backdrop to the news desks. "I sent the crew away except the
technician in the booth and a cameraman. Including the prime-
time anchors. We're just looping the footage of the shootout and
standoff today. So this better be as groundbreaking as you
intimated, Kia, or you'll be stuck in the morgue with the ghouls,
fact-checking stories for the rest of your tenure at WTRL."

His grin confused me. Was he kidding, or was it an actual
threat? Either way, I didn't have to worry since it was every bit as
big as I promised.

He led us into the newsroom and instead of sitting at the news
desks, he instead walked me to the little casual seating area with a
WTRL backdrop where I normally filmed my segments. It had
its two comfortable chairs with a small round table in between
where anchors usually interviewed special guests.

As Bert rolled over the big studio camera with practiced ease, Tobias pointed to where Bert was positioning the camera, and told the ENN cameraman, "You can set up over there." Then to me as he offered me my usual seat, and I sat nervously, "Can I get you anything, Kia? Water, coffee?" He winked at the coffee remark since my two year internship here I thought I was the glorified coffee girl until I learned what he was actually doing all that time in basically making sure of my dedication and commitment to becoming an investigative reporter.

"Coffee," I whispered. "It's been one of the longest days of my life so far."

He nodded and moved to the Craft Services table that was still loaded with snacks and drinks still, the coffee still hot by the steam from the carafe he poured from. Everyone must have cleared out moments before we arrived.

After setting two cups on the little table beside my chair, he went behind the screen and pulled out a third matching chair and arranged the set, then offered the farthest one from me to Lorenzo. The Elf didn't seem to mind.

Then I gleeped when the two cameramen descended upon us. We were mic-ed up and light levels were taken, then Bert slid in the backdrop sign in big three dimensional gold letters that read Killishia's Musings, with WTRL in smaller letters below it. I tried waving him off, "We won't need that, Bert, thanks, this isn't what this is."

He nodded and reached for the sign but Tobias spoke up, "No, leave it, Bert. The viewers are used to it, and the sense of familiarity and reliability with her might temper the seriousness she says she needs to address."

His effort to restrain his little smirk told me that what he said may be true, but that ENN would have it in their frame too. Almost like a poke at the bear, so ENN viewers would know the interview was at our WTRL studio. This man was always playing with a double edged sword , but he has always looked out for me since my Elfing, and I knew it wasn't just because I could pull in ratings with my pointed ears.

His ulterior motives were plain to Lorenzo, who smirked himself, and shook his head slightly in amusement.

As we said a few words each when prompted by the cameramen so they and our technician in the booth could set our sound levels, Tobias prompted, "I assume this about the shootout and standoff?"

I shook my head as I was distractedly giving a tiny wave to Tana, Sofia, and Lisa behind the soundproof, triple pane, viewing window of the newsroom. "No, but as I said, we have lots of footage of that since we were in the vehicle targeted by the mercenaries and Laramer Bloc soldiers. Oh and by the way, the

Project Pelican assholes are back in the picture. And you should be receiving word from the Council about our emergency Security Meeting tonight. I'll write something up on all of whatever I can share."

The man's eyes were so wide I was afraid they might fall out of his head, but that wasn't what had my attention. Lorenzo didn't seem surprised in the least. Did he somehow know everything that happened in the Chamber? How was everything being leaked so quickly to just about everyone? My reporter-y senses were tingling. I knew the man likely already deduced I was a Halfling and this was what this interview was about, but this?

Bert asked, "When do you want to go live, sir?"

"After the next commercial break, Bert."

"We're in one now, sixty seconds."

Tobias nodded and said to me, "I'll make the introduction, then you can make the announcement. But remember, afterwards, you owe me five questions."

I nodded and smirked, "Yes, 'if' I'm allowed to answer." I wasn't born yesterday, and unfortunately I'm learning that there is a price to everything. He just inclined his head then we all settled in our chairs and faced the cameras as Bert started counting down, "Ten, nine, eight..." I took a quick sip of coffee to chase away the dry mouth I always got before going on air. Then Bert stopped counting, showing three, then two, then one finger... then the red indicators on the cameras lit.

I was buzzing with a nervous anxiety that was tying my guts up in knots as my boss started talking in the confident and engaging tone that has won him so many awards in his career as a news anchor and investigative journalist. "Good evening to our viewing public, I'm Tobias Klein, manager of the station here at WTRL News. Instead of our normal prime-time program, we have a special report. We are sharing this WTRL exclusive with a man who needs no introduction, Lorenzo Vasquez of ENN." He motioned to the Elf who was exuding his trademarked brand of swagger as he inclined his head to the cameras.

Then he looked my way, "Senior International Elf Council Member, Killishia Renner-Riicathi, has an official announcement of great importance to share with the world, following which she has agreed to an interview with me, so don't change the channel." He really did have a winning smile that gave him a boyish charm for a fit, middle aged man.

"Killishia?"

It always takes me a moment to get comfortable behind the camera. I know it's not a good thing when that's where an investigative reporter belongs. So I almost kicked myself when I waved at the camera, "Hello everyone." I motioned to my segment's sign. "I know you're used to me doing my segment as I share the ups and downs of learning the ups and downs and ins and outs of being an Elf, after thinking I was Sapien my whole life. But I have something more important to share tonight."

I swallowed and went on, "When I first Elfed, everyone took note of the fact that I wasn't like the Elves everyone was used to seeing." I reached up to take my ear shields off and set them on the table, exposing my half length Elf ears, which I made a show of swiveling as I made a half hearted motion toward them, then to my eyes. "Especially my eyes."

I looked at my hands and wiped at an imaginary spot then looked back up. "The Elf Council thought it prudent to play it down, in fear it would cause... well cause a panic if people knew the truth of it, so they told a fallacy that Elves had variations of eye color, that it was just exceedingly rare for them not to be that cobalt blue everyone is used to seeing."

"I learned the shocking truth about myself early on, but was told that knowledge could make things dangerous for the Aelftus here and around the world, especially in xenophobic regimes like the Laramer Bloc countries."

I took a long deep breath as I prepared to out myself. I centered my resolve then looked up, unashamed as I said while I watched Lisa move into the control room with the technician, as she started pulling something up on her LaunPad, "The events of today's violence has sort of shortened the time-frame of this announcement significantly, now that pictures of the incident today in downtown Manhattan feature other Elves like me which have started flooding the social media metasphere."

We saw on the monitor beside the teleprompter, that Andre's picture was inset in the broadcast, and I was so happy that Lis didn't share Jacob's picture since he was a minor and Deidre would never agree to us sharing information about her children.

I chuckled nervously as shrugged and wrung my fingers just before making jazz hands when I shared, "It turns out I was only half wrong believing I was Sapien my whole life. You see, it turns out one of my parents is Sapien, and the other Aelftus." When I said Sapien, with a gasp of effort I finally repressed my Elf traits successfully, then re-manifested them when I said Aelftus.

Bert was standing up from the camera, eyes wide as saucers as I said without apology, "I was the only known Halfling child until I learned in the last couple days of two other Halflings of the Riicathi clan."

Tobias looked ready to explode off his seat to ask a million and one questions, but restrained himself as he waited for me to finish.

"As far back as Aelftus birth records go, in the past thousand years, there have only ever been two other Halflings, so it was logical to believe I was the only one."

I stood slightly to tuck a leg underneath me and sat on it to tamp down the urge to run away, really fast. "The International Elf Council didn't want to panic Elf detractors, with them thinking interbreeding of the two branches of humans was possible, and would constitute some sort of threat. And I'm here to tell you it isn't. I think sometimes people forget that, as I said, we are all just human, people, all trying to live our lives and find joy and purpose on our short time on Earth with our frends and family, both Sapien and Aelftus."

"As I stated, it is exceedingly rare, five in a thousand years. Most pregnancies from a interracial couple end in miscarriage, and if a child remains viable into the second trimester or later, premature labor and radical complications are often deadly for both the mother and baby."

I had to stop shrugging I realized as I shrugged and shared, "I myself was premature, and both my mother and I almost didn't survive the experience."

Cocking my head at the red eyes of the cameras, I reached a pleading hand out, "So this was pretty much what I wished to share tonight with everyone. I love you all, and pray that people will understand why I didn't share this with you all when I myself found out."

Tobias took my hand that I noted was shaking slightly, why did it feel like I was naked on the screen? He said, "Stay tuned after the commercial break, for WTRL and ENN's exclusive interview with Councilwoman Renner-Riicathi."

A second later, Bert, who had regained his senses, pointed at us then said, "And, clear."

Before I could breathe, Klein was blurting, "Holy shit, Kia! You've been holding out on me!"

I shrank down in my seat and squeaked out, "I'm sorry. I hope you understand why the Council was waiting on divulging it until a better time, when Aelftus relations with the U.S. Government aren't so strained."

He exhaled loudly, "I know." Then he perked up and said with mischief in his tone, "And there's never going to be better relations with Uncle Sam, woman, you know that." He bit his lower lip and chewed on it a moment, "I do believe the Council was right, this is going to cause a shit-storm of unrest among the radical Right, but for the most part, the general public support the Aelftus. And now that there are these other pictures circulating of the other two... Halflings you say? This was the right time to stop wild speculation."

Nodding slowly, he called up to the booth, "Rodriquez, you got any shots of the other halfling? We can..."

I blurted, "No!" Then calmed myself and told him, "He's a minor, and his mother won't allow us to show him nor capitalize on his... disposition." Then I added unnecessarily, "He's just a boy... he only Elfed a few months ago."

He was looking me over again squinting his eyes like he'd see something different that way, "A Halfling. Amazing."

My cheeks burned as I chastised, "Still just Killishia Renner."

He nodded and shrugged, "Of course."

Then we settled in our seats as Bert started counting down. Tobias winged a thumb over toward Lorenzo. "Silent ENN over there doesn't seem surprised in the least," causing the other man to smirk again. I noted the technician was pointing at the incoming call counter next to the window, holy platypus crackers Batman, they were ringing off the hook. And the ratings were skyrocketing higher than my first Killishia's Musings segment had pegged.

Then Tobias was talking when Bert signaled we were live, "Welcome back. Again, I'm Tobias Klein with WTRL News." He indicated the other Elf in the space who added, "And I'm Lorenzo Vasquez with ENN's World Beat, and we're sitting here with Senior International Elf Councilwoman, Killishia Riicathi after her startling revelation that she is one of only a handful of Halflings alive today."

Tobias clenched his jaw even through his smile, not liking the Elf hijacking the broadcast like that. But he smoothly went on, "After that bombshell announcement, let's take some time to ask

her a few questions." He looked my way then cocked a brow as
he realized whatever big questions he had planned before I came
in, had to take a back seat now.

"Councilwoman, you're comfortable I trust?"

I grinned and prompted, "Is that one of your questions?" I
rolled my eyes at myself then just nodded, "As comfortable as I
can be after sharing personal details about my life with like a
gadzillion viewers."

The two men chuckled lightheartedly.

He shook his head, "No. But the circumstances that brought
about your need to divulge your disposition was apparently
prompted in part by the revelation of others like yourself involved
in that dangerous shootout in Manhattan today. Was that incident
connected with the fugitive Sapien terrorist which the Ethiopian
military is demanding the extradition of?"

I started as I looked toward the viewing room, "I'm sorry but I
can't address that until certain papers have been..." Tana was on
her cell, a serious look on her face as she nodded then brightened
as she looked up at me and gave me an enthusiastic thumbs up,
mouthing "Good to go."

"On second thought, it looks like the paperwork has all been
filed. So, yes and no. Yes it had to do with the extradition
request, but no, Deidre James is neither a terrorist, nor a Sapien.
She is an Aelftus citizen who was trying to help Elves who have

been trapped in Ethiopia since the Reveal, out of the country to safety."

I looked from him to the cameras, "The draconian government there is intent on wholesale genocide of the Aelftus trapped there, and have committed numerous atrocities to that end. They didn't want word getting out of what she's witnessed there, which is why they demand her extradition and then sent a squad of mercenaries and Ethiopian soldiers to assassinate her today before we could get her safely to Aelftus soil to provide her sanctuary under the Accords and international law."

Lorenzo prompted, "And there's proof of these allegations?" Causing Tobias to raise an eyebrow at the man. I assume the agreement had been for Tobias to conduct the interview and ENN basically be a witness to it so it would get worldwide coverage.

I nodded, spreading my palms wide, "Yes, not only her eyewitness account of the crimes she observed, but video, audio, pictures and documents. All the evidence has been forwarded to the United Nations, NATO, the U.S. government, and the international courts just minutes ago."

Tobias followed up on my earlier statement, "I'm not familiar with a James Elf family, is it not represented in the International Elf Council?"

He winced minutely when he noticed me put a third finger on my leg as I counted questions. I shook my head. "When Deidre entered Ethiopia to help the stranded Elves, she used a cover name. I am happy to say that I discovered that she is actually of a branch of the Riicathi clan thought long dead."

His eyes widened, but Lorenzo remained unphased, I needed to speak with Evander if this man seemed to know everything already, like he already had all the information. I looked at the cameras with a genuine smile as I said, "My clan grows."

He nodded thoughtfully, "That is good news. After you Elfed you shared that it was believed you and your patents were the last of the Riicathi. In fact, you had been the smallest clan represented in the Council."

Then he seemed to ponder something and made a decision, he made a hand signal to the booth. "WTRL was able to obtain some footage from a security camera on the roof a building at one of the alleys where the violence of today occurred. I know Elves are five to ten percent faster and stronger than Sapiens of the same build. Which is, as our viewers know, is why Elves aren't allowed to participate in professional sports with the unfair physical advantage."

Then on the monitor screen, an inset view from a roof parapet looking down in an alley had me shuddering in memory, though the footage was a little grainy, not being high definition, but we could see part of the shootout. As I seemed to blur, moving faster than it felt I had, the thirty frames per second of the security camera not keeping up with the motion as I was spinning past Tana, twisting us out of the way of incoming gunfire.

I swallowed as he went on, "I've seen Elves moving, but have never seen one move as fast as you did there to save Tanaliashia Laun. Is that because of your, umm, fairly unique circumstance, being a Halfling as you said?"

Shrugging and squinting an eye, I shared, "Probably? Most likely? There are theories that my Halfling physiology has a radical response to large adrenaline amounts in my bloodstream."

I gave him a warning look that he was perhaps over the line with the questions now. He seemed to realize it from my reaction, so looked thoughtful, again gathering his thoughts as he shared, "Amazing."

Unfortunately I could see in his eyes, the hard pressed battle between his reporter instincts and his sense of empathy, had been lost. So as he opened his mouth for more uncomfortable followup on the last question, I smiled toward the cameras before turning to him. "Is that the time? Really? I'm sorry Tobias, but I'm expected in Laun Tower in fifteen minutes. We'll have to cut this a little short."

Then as his mouth worked like a fish out of water, I addressed the viewers. "Thank you for tuning in to WTRL News so I could make my announcement. Each and every one of you is valued by me, and I look forward to seeing you next week for my Musings segment. I'd like to thank our own Tobias Klein of WTRL and Lorenzo Vasquez of ENN for hosting this exclusive special report. I love you all, Killishia out!"

The cameramen looked at each other and the red lights turned off on their cameras. I turned to Mr. Klein as I took off the microphones, "Sorry, sir, but you were getting too close to the line and I knew you were about to double dip there."

He chuckled, "It's the investigative reporter in me. I like this more assertive look on you Kia."

Lorenzo was asking, "This was a wrap, already?"

I accused, "You already knew everything, don't bother denying it, my bullshit meter is finely tuned. Where did you get the information? The Council meeting had just ended and everything was need to know until the paperwork was filed."

He cocked his head and said something he's probably recited in front of a mirror the way he said it so smoothly, "Councilwoman, we're both reporters here, you expect me to divulge my sources? Do I need to remind you about Constitutional protections?"

And before we could spar, the ladies were there, pulling me toward the door. Tana urging me along, "Come on, Killy. We need to get moving before people start gathering here after your bombshell. We'll need to overnight at the Tower tonight, where security can fend people off. Your parents' place won't be secure, and crowds may gather there, so we need to call them in too."

Then to the men she inclined her head, "Gentlemen." And we were off, our security and a stunned looking Sofia leading the way.

Chapter 17 - Raids

It took three days for things to settle back down to some semblance of normal, and I stayed at Tana's place in a guestroom until then. My parents had just opted to stay at my grandparents' like I knew they would. Mom really didn't like being in the tower with so many Council members who she had believed her whole life were trying to hunt her family down.

It was just yesterday when Tana and I were called down to the floor above the legal department, to the security level. I hadn't even known it was there, and the Cookie Twins apparently had desks in the sea of cubicles like at a police station. Again, how had I not known this? They were ever present, and were only relieved one at a time for them to sleep. I already felt guilty enough they had to be a constant presence, but now I felt even worse about it. My guys need a vacation!

We had been visiting with Deidre's children when the call came in, telling us the live satellite feed of Operation Repatriate was prepared, and Charity and Mercy insisted on coming. When Jacob complained, "Hey, why do they get to go? I'm coming too." He was met by a chorus of, "No!" as a kid didn't need to be witnessing the violence that was to come, especially since it was possible his mother could get hurt or worse.

I sighed, closing my eyes, then shared, "Lisa is upstairs with Sonia. Why don't you go watch the Firefly marathon with them? It'll be a blast." He perked up at that and I tried not to grin, the boy was growing a teen sized crush on my best friend, and I was encouraged about his character when he first met Sonia and treated her just like he would everyone else.

His sisters couldn't be stopped from joining us if we tried. They've already proven themselves to have the full range of Riicathi training I lacked. Not just combat, but stealth, infiltration, and the annoying habit of moving quick and silent like my grandparents. Mom told me when she saw them sparring, that in just a few years they'd likely reach master level in Mahta-quárë.

Mom and Grams and Gramps Riicathi thought they were the last masters of the closed fist Aelftus style, but three or four of our newfound clan were at her level and Deidre was on the cusp of becoming a master. Many of them asked me to spar with them in one of the massive gyms in the Tower the past three days, but I declined, letting them know I wasn't trained and Mahta-quárë was beyond my abilities.

One man, Omar, had asked, "But you are Riicathi."

"Yeah, well my fighting instincts are of the 'Run Away' type, and finely honed. Tana and my grandparents have tried training me, just for basic self defense, but we've determined that I'm not much of a fighter. Sorry."

Deidre came to my defense, "Like my Jake, Killishia's Halfling physiology precludes her from dexterous activities." This placated the others though I knew it wasn't entirely true, since Andre was with the Riicathi team that rescued us. And it looks as if he's harnessed the adrenaline fueled agility we have to devastating effect.

I'm sure if I really applied myself, I could get to become passable in combat, but I was comfortable not doling out violence. If fleeing from danger works for me, why mess with it? That's why I have the Cookie Twins, right?

We were brought into a room that looked like the military control rooms you see on television. Complete with huge floor to ceiling screens offering feeds from dozens of body and weapons cameras from the United Nations security forces of multiple nations, NATO units, and ESF... Elvish Special Forces as they staged to execute simultaneous raids on multiple locations in Ethiopia.

Some were at known locations where Elf prisoners were interrogated before their captors tired of them and executed them. A group led by a detachment of Riicathi who insisted on being the ones to liberate the hostages taken in the raid that almost captured Deidre. They were being used as leverage to get her back. She was in charge of that unit under the auspices of the International Elf Council.

There was another Riicathi detachment leading ESF troops and UN support troops that were tasked with repatriating the Elvish remains on display at the military headquarters. That was where the most resistance was expected, and when the UN Security Forces recommended more units, Deidre informed them they were in err.

And here we were, in this big command and control room, with dozens of people coordinating things and relaying info to people in the field, and what looked like a quarter of the Council itself. Evander saw us enter and waved us over to where he, Marcilia, and the Havashires were at the front of the observer group, just behind the commanders.

He said in hushed tones, even though everyone in the room could hear, "They are about to give the order. Deidre Riicathi's group is moving into position now." He indicated a group of screens that were labeled, "Group Echo." I quickly located the camera feed with the Echo One tag and Deidre's name. She was just outside a set of double metal doors of a dilapidated warehouse looking building.

I remember when she told Evander that she and most of the Riicathi were going. He fell short of forbidding it. She had cocked a brow in challenge when she saw it on the tip of his tongue, and she had whispered dangerously to him, "Don't say it, man. We Riicathi are free and do not answer to the Council. We have been doing your job for decades now, protecting the disenfranchised Elves of the world while the Council did nothing. So you cannot stop us from going to finish what we have started."

He started to say, "We didn't even know these Elves were in need of..." He trailed off, knowing that was her point exactly. They should have known, but they had failed these Elves. Aelftus intelligence needed to do a better and more through job after this, to ensure the safety of all Elves. He inclined his head in capitulation.

All our ears swiveled toward where a woman was saying into her headset at the command chairs, "Roger, all teams breach." I noted she was a Sapien in a United Nations uniform, causing me to realize half the commanders were as well, and some in NATO or U.S. military uniforms.

And a cacophony of voices were calling out over the radio links, "Go go go."

At five or six locations, the Ethiopian soldiers were taken completely off guard, not even able to raise their weapons as their locations were swarmed. They surrendered without a shot being fired. But there were a few locations where the breaching teams were in a spray of weapons fire.

My eyes were on two groups of screens, the ones lead by the Riicathi teams. And I witnessed the ruthless violence the Riicathi clan could bring to bear. Most opting to meet the enemy in hand to hand instead of using guns.

I was seeing the lethality Deidre was meting out from her point of view and it was startling the efficiency in which she basically cut a swath though the large number of soldiers who had been ready for an attack. But the soldiers didn't know what they'd be facing. In seconds, the gunfire silenced, Riicathi standing over dozens of dead.

Someone on the team, a French soldier named Matis, gasped out, "Mon deux." While another who's feed I couldn't pick out was echoing, "My god." The Sapien peacemakers in the control room were all gasping. Deidre was signaling, "Echo One, site secure," just as another man was calling out "Gamma One, site secure." I blinked and looked over to see what looked like the military headquarters burning as a team was securing the Plexiglas case containing the Elvish remains. It looked like a battlefield with bodies everywhere, I was so intent on Deidre's team I missed this battle.

I looked back over to Group Echo's feed and had to look back away when I caught sight of the cells that were little more than chain link dog kennels, where perhaps a dozen emaciated Elves of all ages, including children were staring out at their rescuers.

That was bad enough seeing their condition, but what had me trying to prevent dry heaves were the dozens of other, lifeless, Elf bodies stacked in other kennels, dead, sightless eyes staring.

My tendons in my arms were creaking I was making such tight fists. Natalia Havashire reached out and gently took my hands. I nodded and relaxed my fists as Tana rubbed my shoulders. I glanced over and saw Mercy and Charity grinding their teeth in rage.

They had killed so many... just killed them and stacked them so the other prisoners could see.

I learned later that all in all, three hundred and four Elves were saved, along with the Elves in the safehouses and those housing them.

Mass graves of an estimated nine hundred others were found and documented at the military headquarters grounds. Some graves dating back to the military coup after the Reveal according to the condition of the corpses. Some so fresh they hadn't buried them yet.

The Ethiopians lost a hundred and three men in the raids, forty three injured. And the liberating forces suffered two losses, and three Elves were among the thirty wounded. Teams Echo and Gamma suffered no losses and just minor injuries. And sources say the U.S. Military and many other countries' militaries were shocked and wary of the Riicathi and Elvish forces now, after witnessing the brutal efficiency in which the objectives were taken.

Deidre and the rest would be home in the next day or two, after the teams could verify that all Elves in Ethiopia were accounted for. In the mean time... I whispered hoarsely to my girl, "Can I go home now?"

Epilogue

So there we were, back at my place. Mom and Dad got the all clear to head home too and they met us at the door. We shared what we witnessed, and they nodded as if they already knew. Heh, they probably did, now that I'm aware of the network of Whisperers out there.

I noted a much heavier security detail on our block when we arrived and wondered just how long this increased security was going to last. I mean, it was over now wasn't it? Or was it because I revealed myself as a Hafling that they felt tighter security was warranted?

Before we left the Tower for home, Tana informed me, "Father and aunt Natalia have the most trusted Elvish Special Ops members covertly investigating where the leak or leaks are coming from."

"Leaks? Plural?"

She nodded, "It is most likely two separate sources or two working in concert with each other. We originally thought the information leaks originated with the NYPD since we hadn't looped in the UN, NATO, or the U.S. Government yet on the extraction of Deidre, or the planned route."

She shrugged, "But it seems multiple individuals who aren't on the need to know list seemed privy to everything that went on in the emergency security session in the Chamber. Like Lorenzo Vasquez as you told us. He won't talk about it saying he won't disclose his confidential sources."

I cocked my head in thought and nodded slowly, "So it is more likely that there was someone in the Council Chamber, either a member or even security since they were in there. And as you pointed out, someone in NYPD since while the Council knew we were bringing Deidre in, they weren't privy to the timing nor the route."

It was her turn to nod and I mused aloud, "I'll discreetly get with Sofia about it, see if she can't shake a few trees."

This got a raised eyebrow from my girl. "And how do we know that she..."

"Tanny, she's not involved. I know you don't like her, but I trust my gut that she's not involved, and you can't fake her reaction and anger to the ambush." I gave her a patient look and she just smirked and rolled her eyes.

"Fine, Killy. But maybe leave it to Special Ops to investigate..."

"She'll send any other Elf packing since we pretty much make her job that much harder when we hide behind the Reveal Accords any time an Elf is implicated in any of her investigations. She'll give them the old heave ho and be done with them."

"Fine."

I wouldn't even have offered, knowing my Elfette was a wee bit jealous of the Detective even though she had absolutely nothing to be jealous of, but these leaks had just about cost the lot of us our lives that day. I have a vested interest in plugging the leak or leaks too.

As soon as we got home, mom kept us company while dad went to the kitchen, insisting he, "Whip something up," for us to eat since it was past dinner time. We took the time to discuss what my parents and grandparents have been up to while I was sequestered in the Laun's penthouse after my interview on WTRL.

That's when I was surprised when mom said, "My parents weren't with us, they were spearheading one of the Riicathi groups in Ethiopia. The one which hit the Ethiopian Military Headquarters."

"What?! They could have been killed!" My heart was racing even though I knew of all the Riicathi, my grandparents were likely the most dangerous of the lot. But, they were my grandparents and anxiety over the possibility of losing them when I just found them was like a physical vise on my heart.

She assured me, "I couldn't get them to stay twenty some years back, so it would have been useless to get them to stay now. It is who they are, sacrificing themselves to protect others." She said it with an odd mix of emotions coloring her tone and swirling in her blue eyes. I detected pride, sorrow, and a calm resignation in it. I reached over from the couch to place my hand on her arm where she sat in the recliner.

She patted my hand with a smile then asked excitedly, "So what did you girls do for Valentines Day?"

It was my turn to deflate, "Well, we sort of had to postpone. What with Deidre and her kids showing up." I looked at a grinning Tana, who was running her hand though her hair, "The smug one here won't tell me what she has planned... she had to reschedule something for tomorrow."

Mom looked full of mischief, "And what about your plans for her?" She made a silly heartbeat motion with her hands over her chest. Gah, for how awesome mom was, she read way too many of those mushy romance books.

I looked nervously between them and shrugged, "It is virtually impossible to do or get something for a woman who literally has everything. But I think I got her figured out, I've a gift for her upstairs I had hoped on giving her on Valentines Day."

Mom lit up, "Oooo, an intrigue."

And my girl looked with bright eyes like a child on Christmas morning from me to the stairs. I chastised, "Not yet, woman. We're catching up with the 'rents first." She looked so seductively sexy when she pouted.

So we caught up a bit while the house filled with scintillating aromas of Dad's cooking, until he called out, "Dinner is ready. Ladies."

We stepped into the kitchen, and mom moved past us to give him a peck on the lips as she got, not our cheap mismatched plates down, but paper plates when we all laid eyes on one of my favorite guilty pleasures.

He told Tana as mom handed out plates and napkins, "Mediteranian pizza. Special family recipe."

He put out four ice cold lime lager beer bottles as mom prompted us, "Dish up girls. Why don't you scoot upstairs while we go watch Jeapordy."

My cheeks heated, "Moom." She was as bad as Tanny with her curiosity about my gift to my girl. The evil woman was not repentant in the least as my girl took my plate and loaded both plates up with a couple slices each, then snagged my arm as she balanced the two plates on one hand.

I squeaked and snagged two of the lagers as we passed. I rarely ever drink, but these lime lagers were a great compliment to Dad's incomparable pizza. I was blessed to have a world class cook for a dad. He could do so much with so little, and I felt a little spoiled at times when it felt like I was eating above our means.

Squeaking again then calling back, "Help me?"

I got an evil giggle from the woman who had me. "You're on your own, sweetie." I swear she's one of Cthulhu's minions at times. Dad was no help either as he added, "Couldn't stop her if we tried, Itty Bit."

When we got upstairs I stopped her by my door. "Just a second, let me make sure everything is ready." Then I stole a kiss and slipped in. I set the beers down on my dresser and looked at her gift, adjusted it a little then dashed to the closet and pushed my clothing off to one side before retrieving the bottles and hopping on the bed. "Ok, come in."

She slipped in and moved up to me, handing me the plates before going back to shut the door. Then she moved to my window, right past her gift and made sure the curtains were closed. Then she joined me and asked before she took a bite of pizza, moaning in pleasure, "When were the contractors coming to install the white noise curtains in your house?"

I nibbled on a slice and pointed it toward the window, "They were supposed to be here three days ago, but with all the excitement we haven't had a chance to reschedule." She nodded and sighed as she ate. I know she was just as reticent as me to be intimate where all the Elves watching the house and my parents could hear on the few occasions we went past making out here.

I put my plate down on the bed, and took hers from her, but not before she hastily took another huge bite, closing her eyes to enjoy it thoroughly. I grinned and stood, grasping her hands and pulling her to her feet. "You ready for your Valentine?"

She wiggled her brows then said as her bravado slipped and a bashfulness she only showed around me slipped out as she nodded, "Yes."

"Ok, close your eyes." She did so and held her hands out to receive something. I chuckled and just pulled her to beside the window, swallowing as my nerves came crashing down on me in uncertainty that this would be received well. Maybe I could... no, stop it Kia.

I held my breath as I released her and moved to her side. "Ok, open them." I moved my hands up, putting them together and pressing them to my lips in silent prayer as she opened her eyes.

She cocked her head at the antique mini, three drawer dresser that could double as a vanity, with its wood framed oval mirror on top. Even though it was a little rickety, it was artfully painted in winding vines and flowers. I know it wasn't some designer brand or modern chic, but it was what it represented that I hoped would make it priceless to her. She looked from it to me in question.

I shrugged and almost whispered, "It's for your stuff whenever you stay over here." I swallowed, pushing the nerves out of my trembling voice as I turned and raised a hand vaguely toward the closet. "And I made room for you in the closet."

She looked from the dresser to the closet, and her look of confusion slowly morphed into understanding as I blushed, tucking a strand of hair behind my ear as I murmured, "You have a place here, not just in my heart. I just wanted you to know that."

She looked down at me, her eyes, though a little watery, burned with a passion I haven't seen from her before. As she whispered, "I love it, Killishia. And I love you."

I bit my lower lip, eyes wide as I assured her, "And love you Tanaliashia Laun."

And then we were kissing in the most passionate lip lock we have ever shared as my entire body sighed into hers, all the stress of the last few days erased by the inferno of desire inside me for this impossible punk princess who chose me.

And all was right in Queens, if just for the night.

Killishia Out.

The End

Killishia's Musings WTRL Channel 3

Hello, hi... umm... as you all know, I'm Killishia Renner, and this twice a week segment is where I would normally share my thoughts and experiences with you, our viewers, to take you along with me as I navigate this strange new world as, well as an Elf.

But with all the excitement the past few days with the attempted assassination of an Elf right here in Manhattan, the resulting political and military fallout which ensued, then my announcement of my disposition as a Halfling... I haven't had a moment to breathe to prepare a segment today.

But rest assured, I'll be back next week at my regularly scheduled time to share my thoughts on the recent happenings. Until then, I hope to see you on Tuesday for the next Killishia's Musings here on WTRL News 3.

Novels by Erik Schubach

Books in the Worldship Files series...
Leviathan
Firewyrm
Cityships
Morrigan
Changeling
Mutiny
Utopia
Contagion
Underside (coming soon)

Books in the Techromancy Scrolls series...
Adept
Soras
Masquerade
Westlands
Avalon
New Cali
Colossus

Books in the Sparo Rising series...
Blade of Wexbury
Mason of York
Hammers of Flatlash
House of Bexington (coming soon)

Books in the Urban Fairytales series...
Red Hood: The Hunt
Snow: The White Crow
Ella: Cinders and Ash
Rose: Briar's Thorn
Let Down Your Hair
Hair of Gold: Just Right
The Hood of Locksley
Beauty In the Beast
No Place Like Home
Shadow Of The Hook
Armageddon

Books in the New Sentinels series...
Djinn: Cursed
Raven Maid: Out of the Darkness
Fate: No Strings Attached

Open Seas: Just Add Water
Ghost-ish: Lazarus
Anubis: Death's Mistress
Shaytan: The Final Wish

Books in the April series...
Facets of April
Shadows of April (coming soon)

Books in the Drakon series...
Awakening
Dragonfall

Books in the Valkyrie Chronicles series...
Return of the Asgard
Bloodlines
Folkvangr
Seventy Two Hours
Titans

Books in the Tales From Olympus series...
Gods Reunited
Alfheim
Odyssey

Books in the Bridge series...
Trolls
Traitor
Unbroken
Krynn

Books in the Elfed In New York series...
Intern
Riicathi
Magus
Transparency
Fugitive

Books in the Fracture series...
Divergence

Novellas by Erik Schubach

The Hollow

Novellas in the Paranormals series...
Fleas
This Sucks
Jinx (coming soon)

Novellas in the Fixit Adventures...
Fixit
Glitch
Vashon
Descent
Sedition

Novellas in Emily Monroe Is Not The Chosen One...
Night Shift
Unchosen
Rechosen

Novellas in the Shadow of the Scrolls series...
Hell's Gate
Arcadia

Short Stories by Erik Schubach
(These short stories span many different genres)

A Little Favor
Lost in the Woods
MUB
Mirror Mirror On The Wall
Oops!
Rift Jumpers: Faster Than Light
Scythe
Snack Run
Something Pretty

Romance Novels by Erik Schubach

Books in the Music of the Soul universe...
(All books are standalone and can be read in any order)
Music of the Soul
A Deafening Whisper
Dating Game
Karaoke Queen
Silent Bob
Five Feet or Less
Broken Song
Syncopated Rhythm
Progeny
Girl Next Door
Lightning Strikes Twice
June
Dead Shot

Music of the Soul Shorts...
(All short stories are standalone and can be read in any order)

Misadventures of Victoria Davenport: Operation Matchmaker
Wallflower
Accidental Date
Holiday Morsels
What Happened In Vegas?

Books in the London Harmony series...
(All books are standalone and can be read in any order)
Water Gypsy
Feel the Beat
Roctoberfest
Small Fry
Doghouse
Minuette
Squid Hugs
The Pike
Flotilla

Books in the Pike series...
(All books are standalone and can be read in any order)
Ships In The Night
Right To Remain Silent
Evermore
New Beginnings

Books in the Loft series...
(All books are standalone and can be read in any order)
Settling In

Books in the Flotilla series...
(All books are standalone and can be read in any order)
Making Waves
Keeping Time
The Temp
Paying the Toll

Books in the Unleashed series...
Case of the Collie Flour
Case of the Hot Dog
Case of the Gold Retriever
Case of the Great Danish
Case of the Yorkshire Pudding
Case of the Poodle Doodle
Case of the Hound About Town
Case of the Shepherd's Pie
Case of the Bull Doggish
Case of the Dalmatian Salvation
Case of the Irish Sitter
Case of the Pom Poms

Sample chapter of my urban fantasy, SciFi, space opera
Worldship Files: Leviathan

Chapter 1 – Irontown

I navigated my hovering Tac-Bike through the streets of Irontown on C-Ring, Beta-Stack. Another disturbance was reported in the bulkhead corridors. People moved out of the way as my warning beacon strobed. Air traffic was light and I considered heading above street level. This inner ring, like most of the inner rings, was inhabited mostly by Humans and a few unsavories like Sprites, witches, and a few shifters. Which is why I get dispatched here.

I usually get the shit calls, since I was Human too. Why should the Enforcers Brigade be any different than anyone else on the Worldship? Equal opportunity bigotry is the one thing leftover from the old world, that old home called Earth that is just a legend to most of us here on the Leviathan.

I've always thought the stories were just old folktales to keep us lower races in line, that idea that there ever was a place of Open Air, where machines and the ship's oxygen processing systems were not needed to keep us breathing, to keep us alive. But I have questioned it a few times when I've met a couple of the Old Earth Fae who say they were there on the day five thousand years ago when the Leviathan left the orbit of that dying planet.

And Fae... well everyone knows that the Fae cannot lie. Which makes them the best deceivers of all the races, they can spin the truth to make you believe anything they wish and not tell a single lie while doing it. And being in the Brigade, I've seen the outer rings, the lush forests and villages, and rivers that they modeled after Earth. I can almost imagine what it would be like if those forests went on forever instead of being constrained to just a mile wide strip in the fifty-mile diameter torus of the A-Rings.

It is hard to believe that each of the four A-Rings has almost two thousand square miles of space, four times that of the crowded C-Rings. Even more than the surface of the seven-mile diameter asteroid encased in the Heart sphere located... well located in the heart of the Leviathan. The workers and ore extractors there have virtually no gravity, so they can't even come farther out than the small D-Rings without requiring exoskeleton support or magic buffs to support their brittle bone structure in the higher gravity of the spinning rings.

I went past the outer markets then parked and mag-locked my Tactical Bike at one of the many entrances to the labyrinth of corridors, living, and working units of the slums in the bulkhead spaces, assigned to the people who couldn't afford to live outside in the cities and villages crowding the ring's environmental envelope.

An advertisement for cybernetic eye implants was playing across the door, damn taggers with their interactive graffiti were getting so commercial lately. Whatever happened to simple gang tagging or art expressionism? Now it was all about making an extra token chit or two.

I tapped a code on my wrist panel, to inform engineering to come out and strip the programmable paint from the structure as I just shook my head. It's no wonder us humans have such a bad reputation for being slacker trash that's only good for reclamation for fertilizer for the farms, or sucking hard vacuum in space.

It wasn't worth reviewing the surveillance footage to track down the tagger, it was a minor offense and wasn't worth having his or her meal cards set to rationing mode for a month. That sort of thing just promotes the rash of homeless in the lower rings when they can't eat properly to stay healthy enough to work. Not everyone had jobs that made enough chit to supplement their meal cards with fresh food if needed.

Sometimes as an Enforcer, we have to choose our battles. The others from Beta Squad, either call me soft because I let minor infractions like that slide, or null because, like all humans who weren't witches or shifters, had no magic of my own. Ahhh there's that Leviathan bigotry in action again.

Speaking of... a large tiger saw me step into the bulkhead corridors and it hissed and backed off as it changed to human and slipped into a living unit. Ok, maybe the Brigade isn't as popular here in the lower rings as elsewhere on the ship, or 'on the world' as we locals say.

I checked my wrist unit again, and muttered, "Oh go suck vacuum, Bulkhead J?" Of course, it would be the maintenance corridors out by the Skin. I sighed and started jogging through the semi-crowded corridors, people moving aside as I started the quarter-mile journey. I should have just taken my Tac-Bike like the entitled asses of the other squads do, siren wailing and forcing people out of the way.

The deeper I went, the fewer people I passed, until it was only the back hall vagrants. I kicked the hoof of a Satyr just to make sure he was still breathing. What the hells was he doing down here? When he groaned and opened his eyes, he started cursing me in Old Fairy. Who used Old Fairy anymore?

I snapped at him in the same tongue, "Get up, get out, and get sober."

He staggered to his hooves and took the bottle of spirits with him, muttering, "Fuckin' null." Ok, apparently he spoke Ship Common too.

I snorted and sighed, then started jogging toward the reported disturbance. Could they at least have classified it? Was it just someone shitting in the corridor or someone threatening to open a breach in the Skin?

On that thought, I paused at one of the massive breach seal blast doors as I passed from the section, at a sound. I saw flickering lights around the door seams of the emergency manual door release. I stepped over, shook my head then pulled the small door open and growled out, "Hey, get out of there, now! I'll pin your wings and haul your little asses in right now if you don't make yourselves scarce. And hey! Put that linkage back! We'd all be sucking vacuum if there was a meteoroid strike and this section decompressed without us being able to operate the door."

One of the glowing, five-inch tall humanoids with large moth-like wings hissed at me and waved me off. "Get lost, null."

I muttered to myself, "Sprites." Then I said as I pointed back toward the exit, "Out now, you filthy scavengers."

Two of the trio looked up from where they were trying to pull a linkage free, their eyes shooting from my face to my scatter armor to the badge and guns at my waist. They looked at their companion then took flight, leaving a trail of that damn itchy wing dust in their wake.

The third called after them in his... or her... or its squeaky voice; I always got pronoun headache with a three sex-species like Sprites, "Cowards! We can get ten chit for this!" Then it looked at me, harrumphed, then slammed the little access door in my face. The cheeky little shit.

I yanked it open again and the Sprite had the balls to cast at me. I didn't even bother dropping my talisman reinforced visor on my helmet with a thought. The spell sparked from its finger and dissipated against my scatter armor as it lived up to its namesake.

I reached into the box and grabbed the little ass by the wings, pinching them together as I hauled it out to hold up in front of my face. What had it been thinking, even without my armor, Sprites were the bottom of the magic community food chain, right below Faeries. The most it could accomplish against a human is to sting or make a slightly uncomfortable rash with its magic.

I asked as I cocked an eyebrow, "You want me to add assaulting an Enforcer to the list of charges? If you're lucky, they'll have you cleaning out grease traps in the food districts instead of the urinals in the D-Ring."

It swung little fists at my fingers uselessly as it dangled from its wings. "You're like all the other Bigs. If I were your size you'd be quaking in your fancy-schmancy boots like every other man."

"I'm a woman, are you visually impaired as well as stupid?"

It growled, "Man, woman? All you nulls look the same to me."

I sighed and said, "You aren't winning any points here." I scanned it with my wrist unit and an ID popped up. Ah, a third gender, a pollinator, I would have mistaken it for a girl, but I could see the feminine androgyny in it now. "Graz. No surname? You're not that old are you?"

The Fae and other preternatural races became known to the humans of Old Earth when they stepped forward to help construct the Leviathan so that all the races could escape the slowly expanding sun. In those days most preternatural people had only a single name. They didn't start taking surnames until a few hundred years after the Exodus launch to Eridani Prime, the new world our people will call home at the end of our ten thousand year journey.

We were only halfway there, and I and every Human on board would never see it, only the Fae and the Vampires had the chance of seeing the end of our voyage. Us Humans were not blessed with long lives, we burned bright for just around two centuries, then died. So it would still be thirty or forty generations before a human would set foot on the Ground, under Open Air.

It harrumphed and crossed its arms over its chest, and gods be damned if it wasn't cute as hell. "My parents were traditionalists, living on a farm, and couldn't pronounce grass right."

Answered like a true Fae, it wasn't exactly a yes or a no, why were they always so evasive? The lesser Fae could lie, unlike the Greater Fae.

I sighed and said, "I tell you what Graz, I'll overlook your little indiscretions if you just make yourself scarce and promise not to scavenge from critical emergency systems again. I'm on a disturbance call right now back at Bulkhead J, and don't have the time or desire to deal with you too, besides the paperwork is a bitch."

The purplish-pink color drained from Graz's face and it said, "Bulkhead J? The screaming? You don't want to go back there, it's..." The Sprite trailed off, shook its head and asked, "Just... it's better to walk away officer..."

I offered, "Shade, Knith Shade."

"Shade."

Letting the Sprite go, it buzzed its wings to stay in my face and asked, "You're going back there anyway, aren't you?" It actually looked scared... even though it was virtually immortal... well as long as nobody killed it.

I nodded. "It's my job."

The Sprite looked back the way I came as it licked its lips, contemplating my offer. Then it did the last thing I would expect a Sprite, which were flighty annoyances who looked out for only themselves, to do, and said, "I can show you where the screams came from."

Then it added quickly, "Not that I care what happens to another Big. Just if something happens to you, I'm stealing those MMGs you're carrying."

I snorted and patted my stunners, or Magic Mitigating Guns, as I pointed out, "Like you could even lift one, you flying rat."

It buzzed up and sat on my shoulder grabbing the edge of my helmet. "You've got a smart mouth for a Big." Then before I could retort Graz pointed, "That way." Then it muttered, "Shade means nobody." I knew that, but like everyone else, we don't pick our own names.

I sighed then started jogging in the direction it pointed. Gods... I hope nobody from the squad finds out I was taking directions from a Sprite.

See more at...

www.ErikSchubach.com

Made in United States
North Haven, CT
17 February 2024